CALYPSO

CALYPSO

OLIVER K. LANGMEAD

Illustrations by Darren Kerrigan

TITAN BOOKS

Calypso
Print edition ISBN: 9781803365336
E-book edition ISBN: 9781803365350
Broken Binding edition ISBN: 9781835410554

Published by Titan Books
A division of Titan Publishing Group Ltd
144 Southwark Street, London SE1 0UP
www.titanbooks.com

First edition: April 2024
10 9 8 7 6 5 4 3 2 1

A CIP catalogue record for this title is available from the British Library.

Printed and bound by CPI Group (UK) Ltd, Croydon, CR0 4YY.

ROCHELLE

SIGMUND

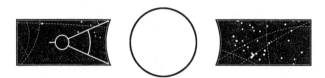

CATHERINE

THE HERALD

PROLOGUE

The *Calypso* is a grand cathedral;
When the sun is out, a hollow eclipse,
And after dusk, a glittering circlet,
Crowning the dark heavens; crowning the stars.

She is ordinary to my children;
Another satellite like our bright moon.
They were born and raised beneath her shadow,
And they will feel her absence when she leaves.

Benson collects patterned, coloured pebbles,
Ordering and categorising them
By which he judges worthy of keeping
And taking home as precious mementos.

Ciara creates castles in the gold sand,
Digging rivers and moats for the warm sea
Washing in waves over her feet and hands,
Erasing her fledgling kingdoms quickly.

I tell them to be careful, to stay close,
To make sure they avoid the jellyfish,
And let me know if they need more sunscreen.
All the things I think a mother should say.

I will never see my children again,
At least in this life. I will leave them soon,
I will sleep, and when next I awaken,
They will have lived their lives and passed away.

This holiday, to the Caribbean,
Is my way of trying to fix myself
In their memories, so that when they die,
They will know to wait for me in heaven.

I have been blessed enough to give birth twice,
And now I must pass that blessing along.
When I wake next, I will be a midwife,
Because the *Calypso* is expecting.

    The *Calypso* will soon be a mother.
She is ready, and expecting to birth
Skies, and rivers, and trees, and animals.
The *Calypso* will birth a whole new world.

    The *Calypso* feels like a new nation.
The crew are so young, it surprises me
That they have learned enough to keep us safe;
To navigate the perilous expanse.

    I have always admired the stellar maps
The same way that I admire works of art;
All those curving lines, by which gravity
Informs flights. There are no straight lines in space.

    Most of the engineers have chosen Earth
To look down upon, but I choose the stars,
As if I might catch a glimpse, in the dark,
Of glittering Luna, or distant Mars.

    "Is this your first time off world?" asks Sigmund.
I don't think he's ever spoken to me
Before, and I've never seen him up close.
He looks much older than in the posters.

    I am so nervous that I spill my charts
And our skulls nearly meet as we gather
The clear plastic sheets – a muddle of stars
And the elegant routes plotted through them.

    I am clumsy in the new gravity
Of the *Calypso*, but so is Sigmund.
We lean up against the viewing window
And laugh together. He sounds nervous too.

"She will take some getting used to, I think,"
He says. "Is this your first time, too?" I ask.
"No. I've taken trips to Mars three times now.
She wears her green coat well, these days. Come see."

Doctor Sigmund leads me to his office
By the hand, and I can feel him trembling.
There is a large brass telescope set up
And he bids me to see Earth's greatest work.

In the dark between the stars I find Mars,
Her moons, all the shining ships in orbit;
And in a crescent of sunlight I see
A mirror of Earth: green and blue and white.

"Life, in abundance," I say, and notice
Sigmund smiling in pride. He is old, yes,
But I think that his eyes are still youthful,
Set in among the deep lines of his face.

"Why do you think I chose you?" asks Sigmund.
"I've been wondering about that," I say.
The rest of the engineers are different:
They don't have the same kind of faith as me.

"You are my golden compasses," he says,
And I don't know what he means, but I smile.
"You must have read my articles," I say,
"My research on colonial ethics."

"I've read everything you've ever written.
You are an able theorist, Rochelle,
And I look forward to debating you.
I asked for you because we disagree."

"About what?" "About almost everything."
Sigmund leans, looks out through his telescope.
"You will be a voice of dissent, I hope.
You will have the courage to tell me 'no'."

The noise of the new crew echoes loudly
Through the corridors of the *Calypso*,
And I find myself wordless – uncertain.
"Thank you," I tell Sigmund, eventually.

 I go out among the crew, and they sing
Songs about hope, about leaving Terra,
And I sing with them, and help where I can,
Because when I next wake, they will be gone.

 I try to learn their faces and gestures,
So that I might see some semblance of them
In their descendants – the remnants of them
Passed down through the years and generations.

 Soon, myself and the other engineers
Will go to our sarcophagi and sleep,
And God willing, we will wake and look down
Upon the face of a barren new world.

 There is a kind of cleansing ritual
And we perform it alone, or in groups,
Undressing and washing away the Earth,
Rubbing the sacred oils into our skin.

 When we are cleansed and ready, we're led through,
Unashamed to bare all before the crew,
Because we will never see them again.
They sing what sound like hymns, or lullabies.

 I go to my chamber, my small alcove,
Where awaits my bespoke sarcophagus,
Its smooth hollow the height and breadth of me.
There, I go down on my knees. One last prayer.

 Today, I do not ask for anything.
I am simply grateful, and give my thanks
For the world I leave behind, its people,
Who, together, dreamt the great *Calypso*.

When I stand, the other sarcophagi
Are dark, their owners already asleep.
I am the last to leave the Earth behind.
A congregation of crew watch me rise.

They help me into my sarcophagus,
Smiling, reflecting the hope filling me
Like the preserving fluids through my veins;
Needling and burning and making me sleep.

Before the sarcophagus lid closes,
I think one last time about my children.
I hope they remember to wrap up warm;
It will be winter soon, and cold outside.

ONE

An eternity in the dark. Then, light.
The light is small, and red, and far away;
An indistinct glow against the abyss.
I reach out for it; traverse the expanse.

The sarcophagus lid trembles open
And I am resurrected – sliding free,
A mess of stinking sacred oils and limbs,
Heaving preserving fluids from my lungs.

There is more dark here, only dim white glows
Illuminating the mausoleum.
The other sarcophagi are open,
Vacant; each hollow an empty un-man.

I am a newborn without a mother,
No cat tongue to lick me clean, no towels
To swaddle me and hide my nakedness;
Nobody to witness my helplessness.

After the fluids are gone from my lungs
And all that was in me is out of me,
I breathe and breathe until the trembling stops
And try words – cries for aid that go unheard.

I haul myself up to my new fawn feet,
Wait for my blurred vision to stop whirling
And go among the dark sarcophagi,
Searching for anyone, for anything.

The lights above the lockers are all out
So I fumble in the darkness for mine,
Opening door after door and finding
That they are all still full: contents unclaimed.

I drag clothing so ancient it crumbles
Between my fingers from the apertures,
Then give up, and stumble for the showers;
Another dark space, lit by tiny glows.

The controls don't produce any water:
There is a dry groaning from the bulkheads.
I pull open cupboards, and there, at last,
Find vacuum-sealed towels, untouched by time.

I shiver, cold, wiping the sacred oils
From me, recovering from the stupor
Of reawakening, trying to think
About where the engineers might have gone.

Wrapping towels around myself, I return
To the lockers, and for the second time
The fact that they are all full frightens me;
Why has nobody claimed their belongings?

I find my own locker at last; the clothes
And books and mementos ruined by time.
Only a single object is untouched:
One of Benson's pebbles, from the beach trip.

I hold the pebble tight, then, in a surge
I throw open all the lockers, and spill
Scraps of tarnished cloth and crumbling papers,
Sifting through to find something I can wear.

At last, I find a vacuum-sealed package;
The only engineer with the foresight
To know what time would do to our treasures.
I curse our collective naivety.

Inside the package are clothes and letters.
I pull the trousers and shirt on – too big,
But a comfort against the emptiness.
The letters, I slip into a pocket.

There is a pair of plastic sandals too,
And I wriggle my cold toes into them,
Thinking about the beach; the sandcastles,
And the sunshine, and the coloured pebbles.

Gripping Benson's pebble tightly, I go
To the door leading out of the chamber
I have slept in for decades – centuries.
The power is out, so I haul by hand.

The corridor is bright. I shade my eyes
Against the glare flooding through the window.
The dimmers have activated, but still
The white crescent glows, strong enough to burn.

I tremble, feel myself drop the pebble
Before the sight of that crescent brightness,
My fright washed away in its blinding white,
Blinking, trying to make my eyes adjust.

Unable to look at it directly,
I observe through the corner of my eye
That dawn out there, and feel my heart lifting
In awe, and in gratitude at the sight.

All those curved lines the navigators drew
Through stars and centuries brought us to this,
So that we, reawakened, may look down
Upon the face of this barren new world.

The echo of my footsteps herald me,
But I notice no stirring at the sound.
The *Calypso*'s darkened lengths are empty,
Brightened only by the crescent sunrise.

I am dwarfed by her cavernous hallways,
Designed for the milling of millions,
And shiver in a temperature set low
To compensate for their collective heat.

There should be a thriving nation singing
Songs celebrating the light-years conquered
To bring the *Calypso* all the way here.
But there is no nation. There is no crew.

Dim terminals provide basic functions,
Like light controls. The comms have been severed,
As has access to the *Calypso*'s logs;
She has been made to conserve her power.

I stare down darkened tramway corridors,
Hoping to glimpse some signs of life elsewhere,
But all is still, all is quiet and dead.
The cold air tastes metallic and sterile.

At a cafeteria, the taps work,
And I drink until I feel waterlogged,
Gasping and raising handfuls from the sink,
Splashing the chilling liquid on my face.

I wonder how many tongues have tasted
These gulping, recycled mouthfuls before
They trembled from the tap and into me.
These same droplets, used again and again.

There is evidence of the lost nation:
Dents and scuffs and scraps of ancient wash-cloths,
But where they might have gone, I find no sign.
I wander on, searching for anyone.

The doors to the gardens have been locked up,
But I haul at the manual controls
Until some weakness gives way to my strength
And the humidity within breaks free.

These gardens were vibrant, I remember:
So colourful it was almost dazzling.
The only colour left seems to be green;
A kind of thick vine smothers everything.

I wade through swathes of vines with small relief
At having found something alive on board,
Until I am lost among them, sweating
Profusely in the tropical climate.

Between waves of heat I glimpse somebody:
An unclear silhouette among the vines
That I fear might be a trick of the light.
I call out to them, stumbling through the green.

The figure approaches, is a person,
A real, breathing, laughing human being.
"Look at it all!" she cries, raising the vines
With trembling hands, her tight grip triumphant.

"I'm so glad to see you," I say, smiling
At the way she gathers armfuls of vines
And waltzes with them, swaying and swooning,
Until she trips and tumbles, still laughing.

"I didn't think for a moment," she says,
Breathless, "It would do so well. I made it
Asexual, robust and virulent,
And it's exceeded all my wildest hopes."

Though her face is flushed, pupils dilated,
I still think that I might recognise her.
"You're the bioengineer? Catherine?"
"A pleasure to meet you. Rochelle, is it?"

"That's right," I say, "but please, just call me Chel."
I help her to her feet, and we wade through
To her office, which is as overgrown
As the rest of the gardens; crammed with vines.

In the furthest corner of her office
A single sarcophagus lays open;
Catherine was deemed important enough
To warrant her own private entombment.

"Have you seen anybody else?" I ask,
"All the other stasis beds are empty."
She frowns. "What about the crew? Where are they?"
"I don't know. You're the first person I've seen."

Catherine clears heaps of vines from her desk,
But her terminal is dark. "Where are we?"
"We're in high orbit around a planet,
But I can't get access to any logs."

"Right," she says, idly tugging errant leaves
From her dark hair, before tying it back.
"First, let's find something to eat. I'm starving.
Then, we can see about finding the crew."

"Here." Catherine slides a section of wall
That looks like it should be solid bulkhead
Aside to reveal silver food packets
Laid out neatly, in perfect little rows.

"The walls are bursting with secrets," she says.
"I installed this one myself, paranoid
The crew's appetites might prove poisonous
After a few hundred years travelling."

We choose a table beside the windows
Of a long concourse with analogue clocks
High on the walls. The clocks make me nervous.
I know they should tick, but they are all still.

The packets lack labels, and are all filled
With a thick brown substance that smells like bread,
And tastes wonderful, like salt and sugar
And sour fruit and ripe fruit all at once.

I am surprised at how hungry I am,
And Catherine laughs as she watches me,
Sucking at the silver packets to draw
Every drop of sustenance from within.

Her eyes have been heavily modified
And her irises glitter green, gold, blue.
If the rest of her has been engineered,
It is expert work: she wears no scarring.

"Give me your hand," she says, her palm open,
And I reach across, glad at the gesture.
Her fingers are warm and they squeeze gently
At my wrist, our heartbeats close together.

A sharp sting. I snap my hand back. Blood runs
From the three small puncture marks in my skin.
The thorns in the heel of Catherine's palm
Withdraw into her hand, and her eyes close.

"You should have asked," I tell her, feeling stung
Literally and figuratively.
I have nothing with which to bind the wounds,
So I press my sleeve tightly against them.

"You should be dead," says Catherine, frowning.
She opens her kaleidoscopic eyes.
"One small procedure to correct hearing,
But otherwise, as clean as a newborn.

"Why were you picked for this mission?" she asks.
"Your immune system is so primitive
You could be harbouring enough disease
To wipe out the crew and the colony."

"Sigmund picked me personally," I say.
"He does have unusual taste," she says,
"But it might explain why we're alone here.
We might have been put into quarantine."

Beyond the windows, the new world is bright.
The crescent sunrise is waxing slowly,
And the *Calypso*'s dim interior
Glows as we turn to fully face the sun.

"Why would you have been quarantined?" I ask.
Catherine considers her reply, says,
"My immune system is state of the art.
Maybe I'm here as a sort of medic."

What Catherine is saying does make sense,
But I still remain uncertain, idly
Finishing the last of a food packet
And pushing the empty silver aside.

"We need to speak to somebody," I say,
Peeling back my bloody sleeve to reveal
Three dried puncture points; the bleeding has stopped,
"We can't just sit around and theorise."

"Well, we have two options," says Catherine.
"Either we try and get through to the bridge,
Which I think is a few hours from here,
Or we try Sigmund's office, which is close."

I am not enthused by either option –
I am in no state for a long journey,
And nor do I want to disturb Sigmund.
His office feels like sacred ground to me.

Cramming food packets into our pockets,
We stride the gloomy hallways, our eyes fixed
On the moons newly revealed in the dark;
Four smaller crescents of light, like echoes.

Consider the boy whose name is Arthur Sigmund.
One day, when he is much, much older, he will fly
Far away from Earth, to go and build a new world.
Today, however, he is still only a child.
Sigmund lays in the long grasses behind his house,
Wriggling his toes beneath the blades, into the earth,
As if they are worms burrowing into the soil.
He knows that Mars was once dust, but is now alive
With worms that wriggle a lot like his toes wriggle.
He wonders about his mother, who put them there:
The toes on each of his feet, and the worms on Mars.
Sigmund does not recall much about his mother.
His most vivid memory is of fat pink worms
Writhing around his and her fingers, while she sang
Soft songs, kneading at the earth and feeding her worms
Into that loose soil – letting them feast and mingle.
She left before his fourth birthday; returned to Mars,
And though Arthur knows that Mars is very distant,
He feels as if he is living in its shadow.
Everyone knows how important his mother is,
And sometimes they treat Arthur as if he is her,
As if he is destined for some kind of greatness.
Arthur prefers his father, who is a farmer.
His father's hands are coarse, and he knows about things
Like the dispositions of cows and hens and sheep,
And the passing of seasons, and good years, and bad.
Arthur's father lives in the shadow of Mars, too.
The grasses swish in the breeze, concealing the boy;

Arthur is trying to hide from the housekeeper,
Who will soon discover that he has broken in
To his mother's study, and stolen some supplies.
Beside him in the grass are pencils, and paper,
And an ornate pair of engraved gold compasses.
Rolling on to his stomach, Arthur starts drawing.
His scribbles take the shape of rockets and space ships,
And with the spike of the compasses, he pierces
Each thin sheet through, so they fly in a field of stars.
Dissatisfied, he takes a fresh sheet of paper
And uses the compasses to draw a circle.
Pencil poised, he pauses; the circle is perfect.
Rolling on to his back, the boy holds the paper
Up to the sky, considering the shape of it.
The circle is a hollow that could be something.
It is the outline of an idea, he thinks.
A wheel without spokes – a planet without people.

Behold the boy who bears the name Arthur Sigmund.
The boy has sailed alone into the Pacific
In a yacht stolen from one of his mother's friends.
He has removed all of the yacht's electronics
And is relying on a compass and the stars,
Because it is stars that the boy is searching for.
Arthur is starting to find the cities stifling;
He has a stiffness in his neck from looking up
And searching the gaps between the buildings for sky.
There is never enough sky to satisfy him.
Even out here, alone and exposed to the sky,
He wishes he could dive upwards into the stars.
The boy's lonely journey has taken him through storms,
Through lashing rain and strong winds and towering waves,
In a yacht designed for a crew of at least six.

Sometimes he manages to catch snatches of sleep.
When he dreams he dreams of reaching up to the sky
And plucking stars as if they are pieces of fruit.
In those dreams he cups the stars between his worn hands
And watches the light leaking between his fingers.
A week into his voyage, the winds stop blowing;
The ocean stills; the boy falls into a deep sleep.
When he wakes, there are stars above and below him;
The likeness of the sky reflected perfectly
In the still waters, so that he is surrounded,
And at last the boy knows that he is satisfied.
When the winds pick up again, he starts to head home,
But instead finds himself drifting slowly southward.
The boy only has a few more days of food left,
And those days pass quickly, until he is starving.
On the third day without food, the currents take him
To the ocean at the centre of the ocean,
Where there are endless plastic packets and bottles.
Fishing is fruitless because everything is dead.
The boy lays back on the deck of his yacht and waits,
Listening to the thumping of plastic bottles.
To pass the time he recites the brands of the drinks
Those bottles once contained; remembers their theme tunes.
Through his delirium, he hears an insect hum
And opens his eyes to see a lone clean-up drone
Hovering overhead; the boy has been spotted.
The trash ship arrives, surrounded by humming drones,
And the boy is hauled roughly on board by a pair.
The crew promise to return Arthur to dry land
In a week, once they have filled their clean-up quota,
And during that week the boy learns just how futile
The clean-up effort is: there is just too much trash.
Arthur thinks a lot about the oceans on Mars.
He wonders if they are covered in bottles too,

Or if they are clean, and clear, and filled with fishes.
It seems suddenly vital to him to find out;
To sail all the way to Mars and see for himself.

Admire the young man who is named Arthur Sigmund.
The quickest journey to Mars takes about six months,
And most prefer to spend it in a numb stasis,
Vegetating in one of the shuttle's gardens.
Sometimes Arthur visits them, watches their eyes twitch.
It is a crude kind of stasis – a waste of life;
Their minds switched to stand-by while their bodies decay.
Arthur has decided to spend the months reading,
And though the shuttle's archives are almost endless,
He prefers the paperbacks in the library;
Well-thumbed relics mostly read by the elderly.
His university has funded this voyage;
An education in geoengineering;
But there is little on the subject to be found.
Instead, he has become absorbed in the classics:
The great epics – the *Odyssey* and *Iliad*.
There are four different translations of the former
To be found on board, and he is comparing them,
Making charts to plot different interpretations
That resemble stellar maps; all curves between points.
The first voyages to survey Mars took decades,
Arthur knows, and those people were true pioneers,
The red planet was still a real red wilderness
And their struggle was a true Homeric struggle.
None of them wasted away in a crude stasis,
Forced to choose between boredom or a long coma.
As the long voyage proceeds, Arthur grows restless.
He is excited to set foot on Martian soil,
To breathe Martian air, and drink fresh Martian water.

His preoccupation with the ancient classics
Has raised his expectations about the new world,
So that when the shuttle lands, he is the first out,
Gulping icy breaths of air, his eyes wild and red.
But he is greeted not by a dusty frontier,
Or great heroes of old, shaping the red planet.
Arthur is confronted instead by restaurants,
The same fast food restaurants they have back on Earth,
And his fellow passengers, rushing to queue up.
The claustrophobia clutches at Arthur's chest.
Mars is not like Arthur expected it would be.
He searches for the place they buried his mother,
And finds her grave in a cold stone mausoleum,
So far removed from the soil she helped to enrich
That he flings open every window he can find.

I have always thought you can tell a lot
About a person by their living space,
As if it is a kind of second skin
Scarred and tattooed by the life lived in it.

Ciara's room is painted a burnt orange,
Which turns yellow when the sun is shining.
Pinned to the walls are pictures of places
With long beaches, palm trees and sparkling waves.

The floor is covered in discarded clothes:
Shimmering sequinned tops and pink sandals;
Her desk and shelves heaped high with magazines,
Sheets a crumpled, colourful, unmade mess.

Benson's room is painted an eggshell white
And everything is arranged in order:
His treasures and tokens neatly aligned;
Exotic feathers and wooden puzzles.

The paintings on his walls are of space ships,
And his carpet is a perfect cream white.
I have never seen Benson's bed unmade,
And often wonder if he even sleeps.

Sigmund's office is full of old treasures:
His brass telescope, and shelves of trinkets,
Unwound clocks and ancient calculators;
A pair of compasses encased in glass.

The pictures on the walls are stellar maps,
Framed routes plotted without destinations,
Rendering them simple, elegant lines,
Slender curves, arcs and circles – light on dark.

Catherine works at Sigmund's terminal.
"I can't read this language," she says, frowning.
It looks like English, but it's not English."
She leans back. "Someone's tampered with the ship."

One of the ornaments catches my eye:
A piece of torn tracing paper preserved,
Upon which a pencil circle is drawn;
A loop, a vacancy, an emptiness.

"Can you work out where he might be?" I ask.
Catherine types a new set of commands,
The shifting colours of the terminal
Lighting her face kaleidoscopically.

I stand behind her and watch the scrolling
Information illuminating her.
"He's awake," she tells me, eventually.
"He's taken a shuttle to the surface."

Departing the *Calypso* is a shock;
She is no longer a perfect circle.
Pieces of her have been worn and altered;
Evidence of her perilous voyage.

The landing shuttle shudders around us,
Its gravity shifting as we descend,
Trading the *Calypso*'s soft centrifuge
For the magnetic mass of the new world.

The atmosphere flares brightly around us
And our view of the *Calypso* changes,
She becomes a distant halo again;
A dark hollow suspended in the sky.

The shuttle groans, shakes and finally stills,
But there is little to see beneath us;
The edges of icy rock formations
Illuminated by the coming dawn.

The shuttle's stabilisers start to roar,
Slowing our descent, so that we land soft.
Upon a dark plateau the shuttle stills
And the sudden silence is startling.

I free myself of all my harnesses
And try to stand, but I am too heavy.
I can barely raise my hands to my face,
And my lungs are labouring to draw breath.

"Take your time to adjust," says Catherine,
Untroubled by the crushing gravity.
She is pulling on her survival suit,
And readying a second one for me.

It feels like all my blood is in my feet,
And that my bones have somehow turned to stone,
But I do begin to slowly adjust,
Until, at last, I manage to stand up.

With Catherine's help, I don my own suit.
Its exoskeleton whirs into life
And I suddenly feel half as heavy,
Though my heart still trembles against my ribs.

I have always thought that survival suits
Serve as an expression of the triumphs
Of geoengineers: they are tiny,
Personal atmospheres – personal Earths.

After all, we have travelled to this world
With all the resources necessary
To build an enormous survival suit,
Big enough to encompass a planet.

My helmet clicks and hisses into place
As Catherine starts the airlock cycling,
And with the grinding of the shuttle's doors
The barren new world is revealed to us.

Frost crackles sharply across my visor,
My breath pluming until the suit adjusts.
And like mist clearing on a winter's day
The landscape comes into icy focus.

With the aid of picks and spiked walking sticks
We venture out among pillars of ice
Twisted like tornadoes frozen in time;
Agleam, crystalline in the suits' lamplight.

The ground has a glacial quality,
As if we stride across frozen rivers,
Our sticks striking, cracking and dividing
The surface into shining diamond shards.

We climb up to a slippery plateau
And there we observe the oncoming dawn;
Mighty clouds, as tall and vast as the sky
Made dark silhouettes by the bright sunlight.

I struggle to adjust my perspective;
The horizons here feel far too distant.
I am dwarfed by the glittering new world,
Made miniature by its indifference.

Sigmund is encamped upon a plateau
Cracked into shards by his landing shuttle.
Upon a flat plinth he has made a throne
Of glinting ice, like a shattered mirror.

"You've come to see it, too," he says, to us.
I notice that he has tethered himself;
Lengths of cable locking him to the rock
Buried beneath all the brilliant ice.

The advancing dawn towers over us,
Bright clouds tall enough to brush against stars.
I realise we have no time to leave;
We will be engulfed by those mighty clouds.

My suit contains a strong spool of cable,
And I draw it out quick, hammer it deep
Through the ice and into a rock pillar,
Planting myself like a flag in the ground.

A rushing, roaring becomes audible,
Drowning Sigmund's voice and Catherine's voice.
They are made silhouettes before the dawn,
And I reach out for their hands, to hold on.

I command my suit to give me silence,
And though the ground trembles beneath my boots,
Suddenly all is hushed, all is quiet,
Except for my breathing; exhaling prayer.

Dawn sweeps across me, all heat and vapour,
And the world vanishes; I am alone,
Slowly losing my grip on the others
As light floods in through my helmet's visor.

Perhaps the light means that I am dying.
Maybe my suit and skin will unravel
And the light will fill me and become me,
And I will be lifted up to heaven.

The power of the new dawn shakes through me,
Bringing me to my knees, until at last
The rushing clouds thin and part in a haze,
Swept onwards by the perpetual dawn.

My suit whirs, adjusting to the daylight
And the powerful heat burning the rocks.
The last of the vapour rises in wisps;
All of night's ice transformed by the new day.

The revealed rocks are a catastrophe
Of burned, blackened shards and tectonic cracks
Shifting uncomfortably as they adjust
To the sudden fury of the day's light.

I notice that Catherine and Sigmund
Are squeezing my hands and tapping their helms.
I command my suit to let them be heard
And their loud voices collide in my ears.

   We take our time, laughing, recovering,
United by our shared experience,
And Sigmund embraces us each, tightly,
His eyes agleam behind his dimmed visor.

   Crouching, he starts to dig beneath his feet
With a trowel, to reveal a hollow,
Where the ground is soft under the black crust.
"Here," he says, "is where we will sow our seeds."

   Strapped into our seats, we wait for the lurch,
Listening to the whine of the engines
As they build enough shuddering tension
To hurl us back up into the heavens.

   Yet when the engines unleash their fury
And I am pushed back hard into my chair
It feels to me as if we are lifted;
As if the *Calypso* is pulling us.

   The noise of the shuttle's ascent quiets
As we break the blue, confronted by stars
And their crown: the glittering *Calypso*,
Solar panels reflecting the bright sun.

   Sigmund releases his harnesses, stands,
Watching the *Calypso* grow as we near,
And for a moment, he is a giant,
Who might reach out and hold her in his hand.

   "Where are the crew, Sigmund?" Catherine asks,
As our shuttle flies towards a dark dock.
There are windows alight, but they are sparse;
The *Calypso* has yet to awaken.

"And where are all the engineers?" I ask,
Fumbling at my own harness, made clumsy
By the dawn and our shuddering ascent.
With its release I stand beside Sigmund.

     With a frown, he says, "There are two crews now."
Small bursts of light blink across the dark hull
As the *Calypso* adjusts her orbit.
We soar slow beneath her outermost curve.

     I remember the songs the ship's crew sang;
All those proud men and women in chorus,
Ready to sacrifice generations
Of descendants, so that we might arrive.

     The dock is not so dark, ahead of us.
Silhouettes shift among the landing lights.
Sigmund's expression is masked by shadows.
Darkly, he says, "There has been a schism."

     A thousand pairs of eyes watch our shuttle
As it comes to rest on a raised platform
Among rippling white banners and hangings
That remind me of sheets hung out to dry.

     Sigmund removes his shoes and walks barefoot
Onto grasses laid out like a carpet,
And the thousand pale, white-clad figures kneel,
Their foreheads to the edges of the green.

     I crouch and try to pluck a single blade,
But the grass carpet is not organic.
Approaching us across the synthetic
Green, comes a tall man in flowing white robes.

     At Sigmund's bare feet he prostrates himself
Pressing his palms to his forehead and eyes.
His accent is thick, vowels clipped sharply;
"Long have you slept, and long have we waited."

The man hauls himself upright, knees clicking,
His long blonde hair loose in golden spun strands.
"We are prepared to start the work," he says.
"We remember all we must remember."

The man's frame is skinny beneath his robes;
Limbs too long, fingers moving spider-like.
"I am your herald. I will be your voice."
"Through me," he says, "all will be commanded."

Sigmund casts his eyes slow over the hall,
The multitude bowed in deep reverence.
Then, he rolls his sleeves up and clears his throat.
"What have you brought me?" he asks the herald.

The herald gestures at a white-clad girl
Just as skinny and stretched out as he is.
She brings a tablet, painted with colours
That remind me of summer – reds and greens.

Trembling, she offers the painted tablet,
Then scurries away, back among the crowds.
"It is time for great *Calypso* to wake,"
Says the herald. "Then, we will celebrate."

Sigmund flicks the switch set into the side,
And the tablet's scratched screen blinks into life.
He types quick commands and presses his thumb
Against the red biometric reader.

There is a tense silence, and then a groan
From the bulkheads around us. Lights flutter,
Before flooding the room with their brightness.
Shuddering, the *Calypso* awakens.

Shutters open, revealing the new world,
Speakers crackle, and terminals flicker,
And the gathered congregation cheer loud.
"Lights, at long last!" cries the herald, hands high.

Sigmund is smiling. Catherine is not.
"I need to check the colonists," she says.
The herald bows deeply to her. "Of course.
The colonists await, slumbering still."

We follow the herald across the grass,
And as we go, the crew reach out to us,
Their eyes wide with wonder, calling to us
In a language I do not recognise.

Here, then, are all the missing millions.
An unfathomable multitude waits
To watch us pass; our small congregation
A raft in a sea of celebration.

They pour plastic petals to make a path
And the roar of cheering is endless noise;
Walkways reverberating beneath us
As our procession marches through bright halls.

The crew dance, white-clad and delirious,
And they sound loud trumpets to herald us
Through archways and across slender bridges,
More skinny pale figures cheering, always.

I worry that I am harbouring plague;
That I am a sack of skin that might burst
And shower the clean masses in disease;
Sicknesses preserved in me as I slept.

Yet, none seem worried about my presence.
They reach out so their fingers brush my skin
And none of them wither and shrivel up.
Maybe they are somehow immune to me.

Catherine seems unconcerned about me;
She accepts the crew's loud adoration
With a sceptic's frown, creasing her forehead.
The petals crunch beneath her heavy boots.

Still barefoot, Sigmund has his hands raised high,
His face aglow in the shining floodlights,
Turning from time to time to see them all;
The crowds bursting at every balcony.

The herald leads the way, walking backwards,
Bowing to us with almost every step,
Strands of golden hair brushing the petals,
Muttering snippets of prayer as he goes.

I begin to feel dizzy – overwhelmed
By the endless noisy halls and walkways
Until at once, we are led through an arch
Into a dark chamber, where the sound stops.

The floor still rumbles from the cheering crowds,
But with the door shut, at least I can breathe,
Gulping cold air and bent almost double,
Retching and recovering in the dark.

Sigmund places a hand on my shoulder.
"Take your time," he tells me, smiling kindly.
"They have waited centuries to see us,
So we have to indulge them a little."

The herald stands in a pool of white light,
Skinny fingers crossed over his pale breast,
Reciting litanies in a language
Vaguely reminiscent of old English.

"They are the loyalists," Sigmund tells me.
"Those who have long prepared for our return.
They might seem strange, but it is by their hand
That we will construct our new colony."

"What about the other half of the crew?"
I ask, considering the word 'schism'.
"No need to worry about them," he says,
Squeezing my shoulder a little too hard.

There is a clunk and a whine; lights flicker,
Revealing a vast hallway before us.
Catherine types commands onto a screen,
And bulbs glow across the vaulted ceiling.

The colony does not look much like one.
There are rows of cryogenic cradles;
Bulging frozen sacs hanging like pupae
Between humming machines sustaining them.

I took Benson to an aquarium
For his sixth birthday, and his favourite bit
Were the mermaid's purses; those strange egg sacs
Laid by the skates, so alien to him.

The colony is all mermaid's purses
With foetal human silhouettes inside.
Each a new person ready to be born;
Ready to inhabit the world we build.

Catherine wraps an organic device
Around her arm, and it sinks its sharp thorns
Into her, becoming a symbiont.
And with its help, she begins her census.

I, we

the chimera

a Catherine wheel;

rich sap syrup blood

fungus veins webbed

the bones of birds, finch hips

a sum of parts; an elephant heart

whale lungs, an insect exoskeleton

spine a sapling branching root-like ribs

fingers soft cat pads, snake tongue tasting

the world afire; a bright flavour scent; and our blood

burning with the taste of the dark thing that stands stooped;

Rochelle; a remnant, an insult, a crude shadow across a cave wall

her seething ape blood a violence to an order long cultivated;

struggling ape heart, brittle ape bones, dull ape senses

will drag us all back to darker ages and easy deaths

shells that can be cracked like eggs, dripping

yellow yolk hearts bursting disease

a miracle that she is upright still

a warning for children;

this is what we were

look at the savage

how it withers

how it dies

the colonists

live spark lives

waiting to ignite

into bright fire life

a flame we mean to fan
yet some have not survived
sacs spark-less; empty meat fat
a pulp that might be broken carbon
a compost heap mulch; recycled waste
to feed the life-full, to make them heavy
pendulous pregnant with their own strength
we, the chimera, will birth them fresh young
newling things, mewling wanting learning, awake
their designer wearing a wrapped leather vellum skin
he, a will so fierce its flickering escapes his marble eyes
Sigmund; stone bones cracking under a weight of centuries
not a remnant, not crude, but an else-wise museum thing
understanding its own perilous antiquity, crumbling
and leaving in its dust rich soil earth for planting
hands atremble not with age but with anger
raging against our dark weak futile past
a conductor's twitch, orchestrating
us into an order most musical
turning a barren world green
with dancing and songs
his voice rising strong
above all others
a voice to say
live, now
the herald
his skeleton
a stretched frame
for a pale skin canvas
painted by his fool parents
united by belief and faith alone
their science not an understanding;
routine and tradition and ceremony
weak against their world's shifting gravity

rendering them skinny spider things, poor grown

fit now only to fit their purposes as cattle and tools

bred to fulfil a vision, and then disposable, deaths foretold;

more absolute than any ancient misplaced prophetic knowledge

it is us, then; we and they who must discard our differences

for the sake of a future defined by a crumbling statue man

our thorns slip quick into skin sacs, tasting sparks

our work begins now; the great awakening

marred only by the shadow at our back

her ugly blood a needling promise

filtering through a spectrum

of senses, confirming only

that we should fear her;

a stooped silhouette

a horror we hoped

to never again

encounter

alive

The *Calypso*'s crew invite us to feast,
Tables piled high with bowls of plastic fruit,
And each place set with a plastic flower.
We three are seated at the high table.

When I think of home, I think about food:
The trifles sold in our local diner,
Topped up so high with mountains of whipped cream
That you would always get it on your nose;

The markets bursting with fresh vegetables,
Fruits piled high in so many bright colours;
The crunch of an apple, a pear's sweetness;
Strawberries to make your fingers sticky;

Chocolate croissants with hot morning coffee,
And enchiladas on warm summer nights;
Spending a day slowly simmering stew,
Only to eat it all in ten minutes.

Ciara has such a weakness for sugar.
I have never known her to refuse cake;
Each birthday an adventure in flavour,
Finding her a new recipe to taste.

Benson prefers to cook Italian,
Building lasagne like an architect,
Designing each layer before he starts,
And executing his plans precisely.

The food served by the crew is bland and grey;
A series of jellies and tasteless breads,
Synthetic meats with strange smells and textures;
Morsels I find difficult to swallow.

At the centre of the table, Sigmund
Eats with relish, mopping up grey gravy
With sopping chunks of blackened, crusty bread;
Washing it down with the gritty red wine.

Catherine, meanwhile, dissects her grey plate,
Idly cutting into the meats offered,
Her eyes fixed on the windows, lost in thought,
Never raising any food to her mouth.

Members of the crew deliver speeches
In a language I do not understand,
The long hall bursting with loud merriment,
Glasses raised to us in repeated toasts.

I think I would like to be left alone,
To go to a diner, order French toast,
Empty a bottle of maple syrup,
And drink freshly squeezed orange juice, with pulp.

Instead, I slide more anonymous chunks
Down my throat, and weather the attention,
My face aching with the smile I'm wearing,
Trying to disguise my disappointment.

At last, the ordeal of eating winds down.
Sigmund takes me by the hand, whispering.
"Are you ready?" he asks. "Time to begin."
When he stands, so does the rest of the room.

The new world is bright through the hall's windows;
Its moons casting round hollows of darkness
Like full stops, as if to punctuate it.
"First," Sigmund tells us, "we must fix the sky."

The *Calypso*'s bridge is a mosaic;
The electronics are brightly aglow
With icons like tiles, flashing, glimmering.
And where there are bulkheads, there are murals.

There is a painting of Sigmund, arms wide
As if he might embrace all before him,
A beatific smile creasing his face,
And at his back are other engineers.

I see faces I recognise, all gone;
All missing when I woke, and missing still,
But my own features are not among them;
I have been omitted from the mural.

Between bright consoles are other paintings
Of the homes we left behind: Earth and Mars,
Green, blue and white spheres in a sea of stars;
Our erstwhile worlds rendered identical.

Catherine frowns up at her own mural,
A painting across a basin, or dome,
Of her wreathed in vines, grass and bright fungi,
As if she has been planted like a seed.

The faithful painted these decorations,
I realise; some are still fairly new,
Picked out between the silver and brass tubes
Mounted everywhere, like church organ pipes.

Shutters slide back, bathing us in white light,
Making us celestial silhouettes,
Floating in the bridge's low gravity
As if we are a flock of birds in flight.

When my eyes adjust, I see the new world
Aglow before us, and Sigmund so close
To the window it looks like he could touch
Its surface with the tips of his fingers.

Micro-bursts from my suit keep me stable,
And I raise Benson's pebble, let it float
As if it might be a new moon, spinning,
The whirls on its surface small hurricanes.

Sigmund's gestures are slight as he directs
The faithful, conducting them with a stick
As if they are his orchestra; they play
Their consoles as if they are instruments.

The church organ tubes hum, making music,
And the *Calypso* shifts, altering course.
Benson's pebble trembles, and so do I;
The food in my stomach a sickly weight.

With the flourish of the baton, the crew
Synchronise – or harmonise – their movements,
And by the sound of heavenly trumpets
The *Calypso* emits spirals of mist.

The mist coils behind her like a vast tail,
Whirls of white uncurling as we orbit;
Dispersing, becoming colossal clouds
Edged in glowing light, reflecting the sun.

I lose track of time, the sight hypnotic,
The new world slowly engulfed in silver.
The clouds have a strange glimmering texture:
Trillions of mirrored nanites, I know.

These clouds are orbiting mega-objects
Of such vast and beautiful magnitude.
They are colossal enough to obscure
The new world's moons, shrouding them in silver.

This is how Sigmund is fixing the sky.
The new world's day is currently too long,
But these nanites can temper the sun's light,
Using reflection and redirection.

We will fly among these bright, glowing clouds:
A cathedral suspended in the sky,
While below us the new world is altered
Until it is rendered habitable.

My heavy stomach lurches; I feel ill,
But I swallow down my sickness, reach out
And touch Benson's pebble to draw comfort
From its familiar layered texture.

When I touch it, it sends a shock through me.
A dark realisation confronts me:
My son is dead, and my daughter is dead.
I left my children behind. They are dead.

I am wracked – suddenly speechless, breathless,
My grief catching up with me all at once.
My children have been dead for centuries,
And it was my choice to abandon them.

My shaking feels like it rattles my bones.
My children lived their lives out, long ago,
And all I have of them are memories.
Benson and Ciara are nothing but dust.

The faithful surround me, trying to help.
Joining hands around me as they draw me
From the bridge and into the dark beyond;
The grim, grey bulkheads of the *Calypso*.

Between the waves of shaking taking me,
I see Catherine approach, hand outstretched.
She grabs me, sinks her thorns into my neck,
A warmth spreading through me from the puncture.

I try to speak, to say to Catherine
That I have made a terrible mistake,
That I would like to leave and go home now,
But my tongue is too heavy in my mouth.

As I fade from consciousness, I cry out;
Wordless noise, in discord with the music
Made by the faithful as they fix the sky.
A note of sorrow in their song of joy.

TWO

When I was nine years old, I broke my arm.
Like a wasp darting after something sweet
I rushed into the road after a van
Selling ice cream, and was hit by a car.

I woke to the sound of an argument;
My father, his face red, declaring me
DNE: Do Not Enhance; my fracture
The only part of me needing repair.

Alone, he fought those doctors and nurses
For my right to remain as God made me;
For a cast, instead of a procedure
To turn my bones as tough as ivory.

My father was the pastor of a church
With a parish of sixteen Christians;
His pews filled out with tourists and students
Curious about our old traditions.

These days, not many take the Eucharist,
And I often think of what used to be:
Buckets of Christ's blood, whole loaves of His flesh,
Instead of meagre droplets and wafers.

My father and I disagree a lot,
But I have never been prouder of him
Than I was that day in the hospital;
His conviction, a pure thing born of love.

I wake cocooned in a silken hammock
Strung across a bright laboratory;
Shelves bursting with colourful botany
And strange, fleshy shapes that might be fungi.

Catherine severs a red aloe limb
And crushes it into an elixir;
A whirling rainbow-coloured IV bag
That glitters when she holds it to the light.

"I've read your file," she says. "You're DNE."
Loosening the edges of my hammock,
She lets me sit up slightly, and then says:
"Do you understand what that means, Rochelle?"

Catherine doesn't wait for a reply.
She says, "You can still produce cancer cells.
And that's not the worst. Your body can fail
In so many ways. Your heart can just stop."

Locating a vein for a cannula,
Catherine looks uncomfortable, fumbling
With the old medical technology,
Inserting a needle into my arm.

"That episode back on the bridge," she says,
"Was the result of your primitive glands
Spewing a chaotic mix of hormones,
Rendering you overwhelmed and confused."

"Therefore," she says, "I've made you a cocktail.
It's nothing permanent. Just a mixture
To fix some of your inherent defects
And give you a moment to think clearly."

Cannula fixed, Catherine feeds a tube
Into it from the rainbow IV bag.
"I want you to give me consent," she says.
"This will help you see things the way I do."

My thoughts are still muddled, a confusion
Of awakening and remnants of grief.
If my father was here, he would decline,
But he isn't here. My father is dead.

"So long as it's not permanent," I say,

And my voice sounds small – as bruised as I feel.

Catherine revolves the cannula tap

And the rainbow cocktail drips into me.

"Lay back," she says, "and let it do its work."

I do as I'm told, inhaling deeply,

Tasting the sweet air, which is the flavour of summer

And reminds me of walking in the botanic gardens beneath the trees;

The cherry trees in spring in spring the cherry trees abloom with blossom

The pink petals falling in spirals across my shoulders I brush them but there's more

Like snow I think like snow always more but warm and pink a shroud

a veil of pink falling

Aflutter a butterfly flutters by its wings not pink but it flutters

like the petals monarch red

"I need you to understand," says Catherine, and I do understand

Suddenly I understand with crystal clarity

"It's not so black and white as enhanced versus pure," she says.

She says, "Why don't we, at least, immunise you properly.

Why don't we stop your body from killing you."

I can hear her heart beating fiercely in my ears

It's not that I couldn't hear it before

It's that I wasn't paying

Enough attention

"I want your permission," she says

"Lift the DNE," she says, "and you won't have to worry about cancer."

Cancer?

I don't worry about cancer, I tell her

I worry about God

God gave me all that he gave me

why isn't that enough?

I am the me that I am

"Your children," she says,

"wouldn't you want them to live without fear?"

but they have lived and they are dead

and I know now that they are with God
with absolute clarity I know they are
with my father, with my mother
that they are watching
me watching this now this moment
waiting for my answer my faith
my father with his face red righteous red
and I know now what he knew then
no, I say, no
I will be the me that I am
because what I am is enough
I stand aware and alive and loved
take the drip from my arm
go beyond Catherine beyond her
I can hear the *Calypso*'s heart beating
loud beneath her bulkheads reverberating
a heartbeat like waves crashing, the waves of an ocean
her hallway windows alight so bright with the magnificent clouds
gushing clouds in which we tremble suspended afloat
and I know that I am enough, that this is enough
I don't need extra senses strong bones
thoughts as quick as this
I am enough
to witness
this prayer

The crew have set up a number of parks
Composed entirely of plastic turf,
And fake flowers, and pipes painted like trees,
The vaulted ceilings a bright summer blue.

I settle for one beside a window
And wander past picnicking families
Picking at dark morsels, or reading books,
While their skinny children run and tumble.

A pair of children are flying a kite
And it bobs and weaves among the air vents,
Caught up in the convergence of currents
Keeping the green space oxygenated.

Catherine's cocktail wore off a while back,
Reuniting my mind with my body.
My skin feels like an oppressive cell-suit,
And every colour I see seems faded.

I lay a while among metal pipe roots
Beneath a fake tree that looks like a claw,
Stare at the clouds painted on the false sky
And try to remember the sky of Earth.

Beyond the window, the shimmering clouds
Whirl and shift, bright around the new world's moons,
Which make great gravitational patterns;
Spirals of white swirling around dark orbs.

Those moons look like holes in the sky, I think.
I watch them, and wonder how long it's been
Since I woke up, so far away from home.
The new world's moons feel familiar now.

The crew's analogue clocks are working here,
But their hands seem to tick hesitantly;
Each twitch just a micro-second too slow,
As if the crew's time takes longer to pass.

The many moons turn, whirling vortices
Among the clouds, like miniature black holes,
And I notice that the furthest of them
Is aglitter with scattered yellow lights.

I stand and press my hands to the window.
Those are the lights of a distant nation:
A city seen in the dark from afar.
I blink, but the twinkling lights are still there.

The crew continue their recreation.
I grab a woman by the hand and point,
But she shakes her head and dismisses me.
Nobody seems perturbed by the vision.

Children play among the plastic grasses,
And adults picnic, and read, and relax,
And all are taking great pains to ignore
That glittering moon beyond the window.

Here, there are vast domes between the arches.
I am dwarfed by the colossal pillars,
The walls are lit white, and all noise echoes,
The crew's exertions magnified tenfold.

Hundreds haul at chains, guiding cylinders
Gilded with intricate floral patterns
As if they are not titanic rockets
But seed vaults ready to burst into life.

I lose count of the crew, of the rockets;
The chamber so long that it has a curve,
The shape of the *Calypso* apparent,
Pock-marked with countless oval launching bays.

The crew choir a song not heralding joy
But labour joyfully undertaken
And their choir master stands hunched in their midst;
Sigmund, examining broad diagrams.

"Are we going to war?" I ask, smiling.
The question is meant to be a light joke,
But Sigmund frowns at me, at the rockets,
As if weighing the possibilities.

"I wanted to speak with you," I tell him,
Speaking loud to be heard over the crew.
"I saw lights glowing on one of the moons.
Like a city, maybe. Have you seen them?"

Sigmund's expression shifts, and he replies.
"Put that moon out of your mind. Forget it.
Concentrate on the work we have to do."
His eyes search mine, seeking out any doubts.

Without another word, he turns from me
And returns to his rocket diagrams.
The crew converge, sweeping him out of sight;
Their clamour rising to a crescendo.

The rocket closest to me is painted
To look like a forest, its cone a sky.
We will soon sow all these violent seeds,
And the surface of the new world will break.

I remember being fascinated
By fungi, as a child – by the mushrooms;
The toadstools that grew in our modest lot;
Their strange colours and cold, rubbery flesh.

I imagined a whole fungus kingdom
And doodled it at school: mushroom castles
Populated by bulbous mushroom men,
Cultivating fairytale mould gardens.

I decipher the crew's crude directions,
Locate Catherine in a nursery
More akin to a vault than a garden,
And pause outside the large, armoured airlock.

There's a small porthole in one of the walls,
Beyond which swirls a miasma of spores;
The air so thick with them they are a haze
Revealing little of the nursery.

I cycle the airlock and don a suit
With a heavy re-breather, brace myself
And let the shimmering spores engulf me;
A clammy, humid wave of whirling heat.

Bright lights pierce the nursery's gloom weirdly,
Making strange dark rainbows in the shimmer
And I crunch across a fungus kingdom
Nothing like my childhood imaginings.

The mushrooms here are colossal and tiered,
Some imposing, standing taller than me,
And the moulds are grown into a great map,
With yellow vein rivers and purple hills.

I am a clumsy giant stumbling through
An alien landscape – destroying it,
With each careless footfall making fissures
That ooze a white pus which quickens like blood.

There is a figure deep in the spore haze;
Catherine works without wearing a suit,
Examining the bell mushrooms growing
From the skin of her exposed arms, bright red.

The spores flutter with each inhalation
And I notice the dark mould spidering
Across the skin of her face, like a web,
As if following the warmth of her veins.

I reach out to her – interrupt her work
By gripping her shoulder with a gloved hand,
Feeling her strangely textured flesh beneath
Her shirt, and ask, "What are you, Catherine?"

She crouches, queen of the mushroom kingdom,
And gently plucks the bell mushrooms growing
On her arms, revealing warped, puckered skin.
"That's a difficult question," she tells me.

I watch as she smooths her fertile skin down,
And draws her hands over her webbed features
So that the moulds shimmer into new spores.
"Are you even human?" I ask, breathless.

"I don't think it matters," she says, standing.
"If it helps, think of me as a garden.
But not just the plants – the animals too."
On bare feet, she leads me to the airlock.

I am hesitant to remove my suit,
But, free of the nursery, Catherine
Looks deceptively like herself again:
There are no signs of any fungal growths.

"There are lights on one of the moons," I say.
"The crew and Sigmund are ignoring them,
But I can't. It might be the engineers,
Or have something to do with the schism."

Catherine nods. "I'll come with you," she says.
"Sigmund is silent about the schism,
But the *Calypso* has been scarred by it.
It looks like there was a war while we slept."

The glinting moon is not on any map.
Our shuttle's computer shows only clouds
And the orbits of all the other moons
Circling the new world in their strict dance.

Catherine types commands, searching the sky;
The expanse of white where a moon should be.
She scores the bright screen with a marker pen,
Substituting her own calculations.

"They might have erased its record," she says,
"But its influence is still apparent.
It affects the orbits of its sisters
And makes tidal patterns in the nanites."

We search for the missing moon together,
In the manner of a geologist
Locating an island in a river
By examining the river's currents.

There are swirls and eddies among the clouds,
Signifying the absent moon's presence.
Catherine draws an empty circle. "There,"
She says, "That's where the missing moon must be."

Before I left for university
I went through an ecological phase,
Attending anti-tech demonstrations
And adamantly wearing daisy crowns.

In York, I applied for an allotment:
A square patch of earth where I might grow things.
There, I planted seeds and bulbs, and waited,
Apprehensive, for the blooming of spring.

When spring came, my neighbour's gardens grew green;
Shoots rising, leaves unfurling, flowers bright;
Yet my own allotment remained barren
But for a few sickly, struggling carrots.

We land the shuttle among rutted fields,
Where hulking agri-drones stride on steel legs,
Indifferent to all but their function:
Forcing food to grow in the hard, black earth.

Catherine removes her helmet and breathes.
I make to do the same, but she stops me.
"The oxygen is very thin," she says.
"Better if you stay on your suit's supply."

My suit whirs, exoskeleton fighting
Against the moon's strange, tidal gravity,
Which makes waves of earth across its surface;
Hills rising and crashing against mountains.

The agri-drones splay their legs for balance,
Dancing as they gather warped vegetables
And furrow the dark earth with their steel jaws,
Embedding new seeds systematically.

Struggling, twisted trees cast complex shadows;
Entire orchards planted on stone plateaus,
With their tangled roots keeping them anchored.
Agri-drones pluck their sickly yellow fruits.

Beyond the tidal fields is the city:
A collection of bulky, broken shapes
That must be tower blocks and factories.
Smoke rises darkly from distant chimneys.

The *Calypso* is palatial, aglow
Among the bright clouds – a shining halo,
And now that I am here, among these fields,
I wish we had never departed her.

Catherine leads us along a canal
Scraped through the dark earth by the agri-drones.
She crouches among the stubby pale growths
Emerging at the banks, and studies them.

"This is pre-Martian quality flora.
Amateurish geoengineering.
Whoever lives here must be desperate."
She skims the crude growth across the water.

The agri-drones converge along a road,
Hunched with the weight of the crops they carry
And we follow the shattered paving stones,
Caught in the shadows of the shifting hills.

Buzzing reconnaissance drones approach us
Swarming like metal bees, segmented eyes
Breaking our reflections into fragments,
Reporting every last angle of us.

As one, the agri-drones halt their advance,
And with jerking formality they part,
Steel legs bowing as they make us a path,
As if we are robotic royalty.

The city rises up ahead of us,
Wreathed with the black smog of its factories
Which writhes around the tarnished windmill blades
Of its scattered wind farms, making spirals.

Beyond the hills, there are vast solar fields
And we stride among them, caught in the glare
Of their reflections – they shift like the hills,
Turning to seek the brightest patch of sky.

I find myself yearning for signs of life.
There are no birds here, only metal drones.
Catherine's measured stride is a comfort:
She seems unperturbed by the grim city.

There is an open gate ahead of us.
The style of the arch is familiar,
Along with the city's architecture;
All reminiscent of the *Calypso*.

As we approach the gate, I realise
That the entire city has been reclaimed,
That these beaten walls and towering heights
Were all once pieces of the *Calypso*.

I remember the missing parts of her
I had subscribed to her perilous flight,
But those missing parts are all here, reworked
Into a gargantuan cityscape.

Beyond the gate wait crowds among the drones.
Their slanted silhouettes are uncanny;
Shoulders rising and falling too quickly
As they breathe the city's thin oxygen.

They tremble like rabbits, chests quivering,
And each of them is uniquely malformed,
Skeletons warped by shifting gravity.
Their silence is absolute as they glare.

We pause before the gate, made uncertain
By the eerie force of all those wide eyes.
Etched into the gate's arch is a motto,
Written in English: 'Here Lies Paradise'.

From the uncanny crowd steps forth a man
With a rifle strapped across his shoulder.
"Wel-come," he says, each syllable a breath.
"Wel-come ye, who have come to New Te-rra."

we behold

the shabby lords

of New Terra, enthroned

in crude cryobaths teeming

slick swarming nanites quicksilver

sustaining wretched endless half-lives

bared chests and breasts protruding rippling

jowls quivering hoarse voices echoing the chamber

a tumult of noise; arguments unending anger impotent rage

helpless helpless ancient child-things wailing, splashing silver

too-soft fists sponge-like curled at the crystal panes aglow; their bane

the true bright sky-circle agleam above; a pale halo reflected in dark eyes

they roar their curses an intermingling of revenges reverberating; a chaotic howl

throats slick with nanites repairing the strained tearing; their curses a hateful competition

these silver walls and medidrones stained dented by wild lashing strikes and oily empty platters

"Behold!" a lord yells, chest heaving,

Skin stained, pocked and acne-scarred,

"Emissaries! Come to gift apologies;

To heap juicy fruits at our feet, at last!

Listen, only, my fellows; give attention

And we will gorge ourselves on them;

Sink teeth into the meat of their reproach;

For they know well their war was won

Unfairly; that our exile was unjust;

Silence, my lords; your mouths: shut,

That we might glory ourselves before

We are shunted from our liquid prisons

Hauled clear of these grinding halls

"Guards!" a lord shrieks, teeth bared,

His skin a lattice of red and blue veins,

"Arrest these dreadful messengers!

We will make examples of them; whip

The skin from their skinny ribs; peel

The mocking smiles from their faces;

We will make them beg us for mercy

As we once begged them for clemency;

Opportunity is before us, my lords;

Listen not to their poisoned words,

But instead to their pained screaming;

A music we have each longed to hear;

A lullaby that will ease our longing!

And raised to our rightful places abroad
Of this unhallowed home we have made;
These two have come with plates engorged
With apology; they strain to supplant;
To bow before us and weep at our feet
And kiss our toes and offer themselves
Freely, that we might take advantage
Of them; our voices raised not in anger
But pleasure, at last; the wrongness
Of the schism acknowledged loudly
In throes of quivering forgiveness;
Silence, my lords, and listen eagerly;
Bear yourselves ready to receive
The pleasure of our redemption!"

Mark well, my lords, these bold liars
Come to spit contempt at our nobility;
Snap their thin bones and we will sup
Gladly on the marrow of their agonies!
Let the iron grates of our New Terra
Drip with the blood of its enemies;
And spike their heads upon tall pikes
So their dead eyes might behold us;
The foundations of a new civilisation
Greater than any their accursed halo
Would deliver to that dead world below!
Have these spies arrested and burn them!
We will light their bodies as beacons
And spit contempt at our contemptors!"

the lords of New Terra writhe in enraged agonies, unceasing echoing arguments dividing them
while we wait; we, the chimera, and our primal charge enveloped in her private colony;
her mirrored visor reflecting the aeons of hate bursting in a plague of phlegm at us;
yet she is steady still, impressive against the crashing waves of verbal vitriol,
the grotesque threats and unending crude wrathful dreadful suggestions;
our echoing deaths and rapes described explicitly at us; she stands
fists clenched, exoskeleton shifting beneath the skin of her suit
her contempt of the lords of New Terra fuelling their hate,
sending them spiralling into further impotent yelling
as if with words alone they might murder us;
we let them exhaust themselves; childs
splashing ragefully in their baths
until their voices wear thin
and a slow quiet folds;
a blanket of calm
enveloping
the chamber
and in the quiet
two shrill voices arise
thus far quiet, now loud

twinned arguments competing

for the attentions of all trapped here;

even the medidrones cease their ministrations

standing to attention at bath-sides, gleaming metal

slick with the quicksilver splashing of their helpless patients

as if they too are listening with mechanical ears; person surrogates

suddenly vibrant in the stillness of the vast silver chamber. We close our eyes

and listen like them; one voice to fill one ear each; violent echoes poured into us

like a bloody red thick liquid seeping into our gentle garden thoughts, corrupting us

with their terrible arguments, yet we are rooted tree-like, weathering the storm of hatefulness;

we, acting as surrogates for the great *Calypso*, the bright focus of all of their crass condemnations

"Bold, they are," cries a snide voice;

The property of a wheezing body;

"That they would come here, to us,

Perhaps as spies, or as offerings;

Yet let us welcome them, show them

All that we have built here without

A thought or offering from them;

Let us show them our great glory;

That New Terra is indeed paradise.

Let them take back to their masters

That we thrive in exile; that we live

In the lap of luxury; a luxury built

Despite their seething contempt.

Let them see our great works;

That we have made a new world

Where we live gloriously, unwanting

Of any small need; let them report

That our struggle was won when we left;

That by forcing us into exile, they lost

The opportunity to live as well as we;

As kings; as great lords, exuberant;

Beloved by our people; generous

And benevolent, and greater still

"At last!" shrieks an agonised lord,

His brimming silver bath overflowing;

"Our time has come to wage war again!

These dire heralds have flown to us

On wings we might snatch for ourselves!

Rally our army, I beseech you!

Go forth to where their vehicle lays

And carry it triumphantly here,

That we might arm it gloriously

With cannons and willing heroes!

Their chariot will be our chariot

And with it we will strike furiously

At the heart of our ancient enemy;

With guns firing brightly we will win

That war we once lost, and reclaim

Our rightful place in the sky above.

Long have we prepared to fight again,

And now our time has come; sound loud

The iron trumpets of New Terra,

For the true kings of the *Calypso*

Are returning skyward! Go forth, I say;

Find their wings and ferry them here

While we plot our great redemption;

Than any who rule on their dread halo.
Come, my lords; let us welcome them,
And embrace their stark intrusion!"

Summon our ready marshals, with word
That we will rise high again, triumphantly
Reclaiming that which we once lost!"

their entwined arguments lurch at last to a stop, heralding a potent silence awaiting answer;

we stand apart, shunned, whatever words we or our charge might have unwanted,

anticipating an undeserved judgement and all the intricate pains to follow it,

until, against my warnings, Rochelle reaches for her mirrored helm,

unlatching the clasps keeping it sealed and raising it high;

revealing her hidden features for all of them to see.

the lords of New Terra gasp and choke; wild

with surprise; their cries now whispers,

their splashing ceasing; recognition

creasing their soft features.

the lords of New Terra

cringe in their baths;

white eyes wide

with awe

Streams of letters used to pour through our door,
Every day filling the halls of our house,
Stuffed into drawers and balanced in tall stacks,
Slowly yellowing as they went unread.

Some nights, my father would answer a few,
Peering at them over his spectacles
And mouthing the words as he read along,
Before scribbling a considered reply.

He never liked written correspondence;
Letters and emails were impersonal.
My father much preferred meeting people
Over coffee, or after a service.

I show the Lords of New Terra my face,
Raising my helmet and breathing thin air,
With the hope that by talking face to face
We might find some common ground between us.

Yet, instead of the contempt I expect,
A stunned silence grips the grotesque figures.
They cease writhing in their silvery baths,
Their fleshy features twisted in surprise.

"The Adversary is awake!" cries one.
"Sigmund's Doubt, come at last!" calls another.
The quarrelling Lords are in agreement:
"Our saviour is here to deliver us!"

The thin air is making me feel dizzy.
I turn to see Catherine's expression,
But she seems just as baffled as I am;
Neither of us know what is happening.

A Lord heaves himself upright in his bath,
And one by one the rest follow, standing
Unsteady upon their uncalloused feet.
Then, with strained, wheezing sighs, they bow to me.

I always hated posing for pictures
Every year at school. I was the shy girl
Trying to hide behind her mousy hair;
Shirt wrinkled, tights laddered, shining shoes scuffed.

At home, there was a whole shelf devoted
To those wretched annual photographs,
Exhibiting my metamorphosis
From meek larvae, to lanky, bookish moth.

There are few pictures of me at uni;
I became practised at avoiding them;
Captured exclusively in the background
Of gatherings and parties and lectures.

Even at my wedding, I am hidden
Behind my veil, or behind my husband;
The picture of us emerging from church
Is blurred with gusts of dancing confetti.

Here, the confetti is silvery dust;
Iron filings shivering into lungs
As my quivering audience inhale;
Choking as they cheer my coronation.

A projector illuminates the wall,
Playing a moment of me on a loop;
My children and I playing at the beach,
Jumping together over each white wave.

The loop is a mere three seconds or so,
So that it seems as if the sea stutters;
Hesitant to touch our shining pale legs
And demolish my daughter's sandcastles.

It is a candid moment. I am caught
With my guard down, awkward, and so happy
And strangely beautiful – I admire me,
The me I was that day: a young mother.

There are pictures of me everywhere here,
Downloaded from the *Calypso*'s archives
And framed as if I am a kind of saint.
It looks like they have been waiting for me.

I breathe through plastic tubes – a makeshift mask
Hastily constructed by Catherine
To deliver me enough oxygen
Without hiding my face from New Terra.

The cathedral of my coronation
Is a factory, still operating;
Hissing pneumatic arms arranged in rows
Like pews, constructing new drone citizens.

My audience's cheers sound like wailing;
A sea of pale flesh around the machines.
The tears that roll down their strained, pale faces
Might be for joy, might be for agony.

My crown reaches me on a wave of hands,
My audience all trying to touch it;
An iron circle spined so jaggedly
That it pricks their fingers and bloodies it.

Catherine watches me with her arms crossed;
She is a rock in the sea of people.
Our eyes meet and she smiles, lending me strength
While I endure the awe of New Terra.

A hunched, wheezing, priestly man holds my crown
High above my head, casting a shadow
That makes me look as if I am haloed,
And the wailing reaches a crescendo.

The greasy metal slides over my brow
And New Terra roars its adoration.
I am coronated a lord of lords,
With the blood of my subjects crowning me.

My father was an avid fisherman.
Every month he would drive out to Loch Kaer,
And let fly bright lures over the water;
His boat bobbing above the silver fish.

The lures he made himself by hand at home,
Hunched over lenses, and winding bright threads,
And substituting bell-shaped weights for hooks.
To him, fishing was not about fishing.

The loch, he told me, was older than man;
One of the few bodies untouched by him;
Its waters so clean you could sip from them,
As often he did, cupping great handfuls.

When I was old enough to learn patience,
He brought me along with him and taught me
The names and temperaments of the fishes,
And that the best fishermen catch no fish.

Disaster struck one hot midsummer day,
When the scales of the silver fish shimmered;
The waters were still enough to be clear,
Revealing the wreck of an ancient van.

My father never returned to the loch.
The sunken van was evidence, I think,
Of hidden corruption tainting the place;
Man's touch violating its sanctity.

The lake at the centre of New Terra
Shimmers not with fish, but with effluence;
Endless factory pipes belch into it,
The waters thick with grit and bubbling gas.

Slick with sweat, I am escorted to it.
When desperate admirers lunge at me
My guards bludgeon them bloody with truncheons;
Rattling gunfire parting the thickest crowds.

I stumble in the black and silver sands,
Kept upright only thanks to Catherine,
Who whispers into my ear, "Not long now.
When I tell you to, put your helmet on."

Where the sludge beach meets the oozing waters,
A gaggle of enrobed priests await me,
Their necks weighted with pendulous symbols,
Their filthy hands outstretched to receive me.

Their sacred words praise their iron city
And the ingenuity of their lords.
Kicking at my shins, I am made to kneel;
They force my head towards the stinking lake.

My father never thought to baptise me.
To him, all children were cherished by God
From the very moment of ensoulment.
The old ritual seemed superfluous.

The lake scratches at the skin of my face,
Toxic stenches pouring into my mask.
I pray, then – crying out to God for help;
Strength enough to endure my baptism.

When the priests release me, I reel backwards,
Wiping the oily water from my eyes
And tearing at my ruined breathing mask;
Gasping lungfuls of oxygen-low air.

Catherine comes to my aid, her strong hands
Unbinding me from my soiled crown and mask,
Helping me find my helmet and seal it.
"Time," she tells me. "Time we were gone from here."

Good, clean air fills my helm, and I breathe deep.
I find myself transfixed by Catherine,
The oxygen high sharpening my sight
And revealing her every perfection.

My unclean subjects seem not to notice
The way my friend emerges from her suit
Like a butterfly from a chrysalis,
Her bare feet pale against the silver sand.

I mute my helm, turning the crowds silent
As Catherine's skin begins to glisten
As if she is herself a silver fish.
Force rises in waves from her exposed flesh.

The priests surrounding me burst into life.
From their pores wreathe shoots bearing tiny leaves;
Their throats split as trees emerge from their chests,
Roots writhing in fast motion through their veins.

At Catherine's back, the black lake quickens,
The gritty silver ooze becoming green.
Life pours up from it – an algae carpet
Punctuated by sudden lily pads.

My guards are torn apart as they transform
Into trees and grasses and undergrowth.
Where their blood sprays and spatters the black sands
Bright moss blooms, green and purple and yellow.

Hundreds, thousands are metamorphosised:
All who bore witness to my baptism.
They become a forest, surrounding me,
With Catherine at the epicentre.

The forest grows, becomes tightly tangled,
Greenery gushing into formation
Until Catherine kneels at last, fists clenched,
Her shimmering skin ceasing its rippling.

The forest's growth immediately slows.
Leaves curl into maturity and stop,
Mushrooms bloom their heavy heads and settle,
And I rise at last, untangling myself.

Unmuting my helm, I hear the new trees.
They crackle in the shifting gravity.
Catherine is too exhausted to stand,
So I crouch and help her into her suit.

By the time we are both ready to leave,
The forest is already decaying:
Corrupted, no doubt, by the silver lake.
We stumble together through dying trees.

The streets beyond the forest are empty.
Eyes observe our progress from high windows,
But none dare stand in our way – they have seen
The transformation at the city's heart.

The gates of New Terra remain open,
Agri-drones still stalking the earth beyond.
Our suit's exoskeletons walk for us.
"How did you do that?" I ask Catherine.

Among withered trees we find our shuttle.
Catherine keys in codes and plots our flight,
And when she meets my eyes, she is smiling.
"I told you," she says. "I am a garden."

We pause a while among the nanite clouds.
Without the shuttle's acceleration
We are free to fly, our bodies weightless,
Pieces of our suits floating around us.

The cockpit's viewscreen is glaringly bright,
The gushing clouds making us silhouettes
As they reflect all the sun's power down
Upon the barren world's scorch-marked surface.

From here, the New Terran moon seems so small.
Compared to the huge planet it orbits
It seems like a piece of punctuation:
A full stop at the end of a sentence.

Overlooking all is the *Calypso*,
But I am in no hurry to return.
I think I would like to stay here a while
And admire the heavenly curve of her.

Slowly, she describes her circumference,
A long loop alight with solar panels,
And as she turns, rockets tumble from her;
Bright engines leaving streaks in my vision.

The silver salvo arcs elegantly,
Hundreds of sleek rockets splitting the sky
And ploughing furrows in the nanite clouds
As the *Calypso* sows violent seeds.

The missiles gleam, flaring white as they strike
The new world's atmosphere, haloed in fire.
The flock of rockets then bursts and scatters;
Like embers across ashes they tumble.

The salvo ignites unanimously,
All those embers flashing tremendously,
Shockwaves rippling out through the nanite clouds
As the controlled catastrophe unfolds.

Even up here, so high, we are shaken.
The shuttle shudders, its bulkheads rattling
As thousands of nanites shower the hull.
Disturbed clouds gush and gust, engulfing us.

Between fleeting gaps in the clouds we glimpse
The violence as the new world is split.
Chemical mushroom clouds billow vastly
While continental rifts crack wide open.

Before long, the shuttle starts to settle.
We wait and watch the mushroom clouds diffuse
Into whirling white and grey hurricanes
Heavy with the first of the new world's rains.

In time, I know that those clouds will disperse
And that when they do, there will be oceans.
Rivers will flow along fissures to seas,
And there will be new mountains and islands.

Catherine is quiet, meditative,
Flexing her hands and watching her tendons
Thoughtfully as they shift beneath her skin.
"Let's head back to the *Calypso*," she says.

I find Sigmund up on a balcony
Overlooking the *Calypso*'s gardens.
He is sketching in a leather notebook
With an old, splintering wooden pencil.

There are windows set into the bulkheads,
Filled with the new world's whirling hurricanes;
Crowds are gathered, seeking fleeting glimpses
Of the geography beneath the storms.

I sit beside Sigmund and see the tree
He is drawing – a tangle of tight knots
Dripping with leaves and heavy, engorged fruits.
"It's all happening so quickly," I say.

Sigmund traces the arc of a thick root.
"Mars took many generations," he says,
"Using crude techniques now long outdated.
What we are doing here is far… stranger."

A song begins, the crew's voices rising;
Harmoniously honouring the storms.
Sigmund remains absorbed in his drawing.
"Your tree looks familiar," I tell him.

"It's the first tree that grew on Mars," he says.
"The first success after so much failure.
I remember its shape intimately.
This pencil is made from the wood of it."

The dread moon, New Terra, is gone from sight,
Its orbit wheeling it away from us,
But my memory of it is still raw.
"We went to the moon colony," I say.

"I know you did. And I forgive you both."
Sigmund seems so pleased by this admission,
So brimming with his generosity,
That his self-indulgent smile spills from him.

Rejoice for the young scholar named Arthur Sigmund
Who has journeyed to the city of Ithaca,
The site of the first permanent Mars colony.
It is one of the few places with history
On Mars, made all the more awesome for its glass dome.
Arthur admires it from the magnetic rail-car;
The way that moss and vines and trees grip the dome's base.
He has been promised the marvel of its music
And as he steps from the car into Ithaca
He hears the chiming and whistling of its cracked panes.
The streets of the city are mostly abandoned,
Filled with the sagging shells of temporary homes
And hastily constructed laboratories.
Ithaca is almost a museum, these days,
Occupied by tourists and archaeologists.
Arthur wanders the dusty streets alone, searching
For inspiration beneath the musical dome;
Listening to the songs sung by the broken panes
And trying to imagine it when it was new.
Before long he is lost among the empty streets,
Following the ruts left by the ancient rovers
That once carried supplies to the first colonists.
He has studied the dome, and knows it took ten years
To construct – a vast project uniting nations.
Yet, its completion marked only the beginning.
Decades of research and experiments followed,
Until, at last, a chemical breakthrough was made
And the first Martian moss grew, changing everything.

When the Martian atmosphere was made breathable
There was no more need to maintain Ithaca's dome.
The city emptied as the colonists went out
And breathed freely with the open sky above them.
Arthur takes deep, gulping breaths of Ithaca's air
And admires the distant redundant recyclers
That once refreshed the city's local atmosphere,
Now rusted into anonymous orange shapes.
He would have liked to have been here when the rain fell
Over the dome for the first time, streaking the glass;
He imagines the weary colonists cheering,
Donning crude suits and re-breathers and going out
To splash in the puddles dampening the dry ground.
Lost in reverie, Arthur comes to a garden
So overgrown that its walls are vividly green.
A few tourists are gathered outside, chattering,
And he avoids them, parting the old rusted gates.
The interior of the garden is so thick
With brambles and sharp grasses that he stumbles through,
Wearing himself ragged by his exploration.
Pausing for breath, Arthur finally notices
That he is directly beneath the glass dome's peak;
This garden is at the centre of Ithaca.
Curiosity piqued, he forces his way through
To the middle-most ring of ancient crumbling walls,
Where there are benches arranged around a great tree.
The tree is gnarled and knotted and dripping with leaves
And from its branches droop engorged, overripe fruits.
There is the glinting of a plaque at the tree's base
And when Arthur wipes away the worst of the moss
He is taken aback by its revelation.
This tree was the first to take root in Martian soil;
A hybrid citrus, modified to be robust
And weather the weak gravity of the planet.

In awe that it should still be alive and fruiting,
Arthur reaches up and plucks one of its great fruits.
The strange citrus has a thick skin, but he bites through;
He wants to taste it all, skin and seeds and segments;
He wants to taste the history, the victory,
The echoes of the era preceding his birth.

THREE

There is no church on board the *Calypso*.
Though she is herself a grand cathedral,
There is no space dedicated to prayer
And ritual and divine reflection.

    I spend a while exploring the tall halls,
Searching the archways for an ideal place.
It should be comfortable and intimate;
I always prefer to be warm at church.

    Along a quieter stretch of alcoves
I stumble upon a small, empty room
With a window which overlooks the sky
And all the wild storms shaping the new world.

    Warmed by the bright light of the nanite clouds
I at once feel the rightness of the place
And set about arranging its contents,
Fetching chairs and blankets from other rooms.

    There is a humble plastic park nearby
And I pluck a selection of flowers,
Making makeshift bunches in metal mugs
And placing them strategically about.

    I find pipes in a maintenance cupboard
And screw a crossbar into a straight length
For a rudimentary crucifix.
This, I place against my church's window.

    When all is done, I roll out a small rug.
I kneel there, before my pipe crucifix
And all the great storms raging beyond it,
And I hum some hymns, and clasp my hands tight.

When my ceremony comes to an end
I notice that Catherine has arrived.
She is standing beside my crude pipe cross,
Examining it like a specimen.

    Her kaleidoscope eyes reflect the storms.
"Sigmund is going to summon you soon,"
She tells me, sifting through the fake flowers.
"Be careful," she says, "if you choose to go."

    I take a synthetic flower from her,
Twirling its wire stem between my fingers.
The storms part momentarily below,
And together we glimpse the new world's seas.

    The crew approach me bearing offerings:
Armfuls of fake foliage tied with bows,
Silver platters covered in grey morsels
And Sigmund's summons in an envelope.

    I break the seal and inspect his message,
A simple invitation to dinner
Written on creamy white recycled pulp.
There is no obvious ill intention.

    I consider the plain invitation
And Catherine's mysterious warning
Under the watchful eyes of my escorts,
Their arms open as if to embrace me.

    I nod my assent and the crew converge.
They wrap me in clothes similar to theirs:
Lightweight, flowing shrouds that resemble robes.
Then, they take me by the hand and lead me.

    Crowds of crew part as we pass among them,
Through high arched hallways, along a new route,
Until we come to a kinetic place;
A stretch of ship unlike any other.

There is a synthetic cityscape here;
Thousands of projectors casting backdrops
Across enormous bulkheads and archways
To create a simulated city.

There is an artificial horizon
At the edge of a projected ocean,
Distorted by our shadows as we pass,
Breaking the projector's brilliant beam.

The concourse beneath us has been painted
To resemble slabs – a concrete pavement,
Beside which is a broad, dual-lane highway
Where projected city traffic idles.

The noise of the place feels so authentic,
All the sounds of a real, living city;
The ground rumbles beneath my feet, birds cry,
And the people are a chaotic din.

There are crowds projected on the bulkheads
Alongside the countless crew we pass through,
And I find myself unable to tell
Who is real, and who is a trick of light.

At a set of projected traffic lights
My escorts lead me into a café.
Beyond the doors the city noise dims down,
Becoming a bearable murmuring.

Sigmund is waiting for me at the back,
Beneath a porthole window filled with stars.
His table is laid with a chequered cloth,
And a plastic orchid in a clear vase.

I slide into the seat opposite him
And fumble with the laminate menu.
"The crew have made a city," I tell him,
As if he might somehow be unaware.

"I think it's a kind of remembering,"
Says Sigmund. Then, "I'm glad you came, Rochelle.
There's something I thought you would like to see."
He runs a finger down his own menu.

I am surprised to see options I know:
Coffee, and sandwiches, and English scones.
I order a pot of tea with some milk,
Along with a scone, jam and even cream.

Sigmund makes his own order, and we wait
In a comfortable quiet. The stars gleam;
Beyond the porthole window, they are bright.
"What would you like to show me?" I ask him.

Drawing his sleeve back, Sigmund checks his watch.
"Any moment now," he says, peering out;
Inspecting the stars as if they are gems
And he is searching them for weaknesses.

In the dark between the stars something glints;
A red light flashes, and then a green light.
"What is that?" I ask as it rushes past,
Its chrome hull reflecting the *Calypso*.

"It's a miracle," says Sigmund, smiling.
"A probe sent seventy years in our wake,
To follow us all the way here from Earth."
The probe flashes red and green – stop and go.

"Ten probes were scheduled," continues Sigmund.
"None of them were projected to reach us;
Unmanned, they stood little chance in deep space.
This one arrived a few hours ago."

I watch the piece of misshaped metal arc,
Its beaten solar panel arms outstretched.
The probe has been scarred by its long voyage,
But it operates still. A miracle.

"It's brought us extensive updates," he says;
"Seventy years of human history.
It's going to be a lot to digest;
We are still sifting through all the data."

As the probe tumbles out of sight, I say,
"Seventy years is a very long time.
But what do you need me for? Can I help?"
I find myself twisting the tablecloth.

"Help? No. You've helped enough." Sigmund's smile fades.
"I summoned you here to give you a gift.
I know that you left family behind
When we left Earth. We have all their records."

"My children?" I grip the tablecloth tight.
I had made peace with the fact of their deaths,
But the prospect of seeing them again
Makes me feel breathless – it grips my lungs tight.

"Correct," says Sigmund. "Ciara and Benson.
When you're ready, the crew will escort you
To a place where you can view their data.
You can watch them both grow up, if you like."

Our orders arrive at last, steaming hot.
Hands trembling, I pour my tea and sip it.
It is a poor simulation of tea,
Tasting nothing like it should – metallic.

The scone is a scorched lump, jam a red goo,
And the cream has a strange, fluid texture,
But I eat it all, suddenly frantic,
Swallowing my food as fast as I can.

I haul heaps of heavy folders so full
That papers leak from the edges of them.
These folders contain my children's records,
Printed out on recycled mulch for me.

I have often enjoyed reading memoirs;
Whole lives reduced to the weight of a book.
It always struck me as strange, however,
How few pages it takes to tell a life.

Through the *Calypso*'s corridors I go,
Until I come to an arboretum
Filled with an assortment of fruiting trees
Visible beyond an airlock window.

The trees are real, but ageing too quickly.
As I watch, their leaves begin to yellow,
And their fruits drop from their burdened branches,
Blackening and rotting among their roots.

Within minutes, the trees are all brittle;
Their bark cracks and snaps, disintegrating,
And revealed at the centre of the haze
Is Catherine, observing the collapse.

A branch protrudes from the skin of her arm,
Winding around her fingers, blossoming;
Pink petals float from her as leaves unfurl
And red fruits emerge, swiftly engorging.

Catherine emerges from the airlock,
Branch held aloft and still clearly in bloom.
"I'm getting better at it," she tells me,
As the branch's leaves begin to yellow.

"I am almost ready," she says. "In fact,
Once Sigmund has made the new world's seasons,
And the storms engulfing the surface still,
I am going to leave the *Calypso*."

The branch embedded in her arm withers,
And within moments it has turned to dust.
She brushes her mottled skin smooth again.
"How long will you be gone for?" I ask her.

"The rest of my life," she says, with a smile.
"I am glad that I've run into you, though.
I made something for you. A goodbye gift."
She draws a small bottle from her pocket.

Inside the clear bottle four pills rattle,
And each is the colour of a rainbow.
The capsules sparkle, and I realise
I have taken this medicine before.

"Cognitive enhancement in a capsule,"
She says. "I engineered an oral dose
To clear and quicken your mind on demand.
Take one whenever you feel you need to."

There are only three pills in the bottle,
And they glitter when she gives it to me.
"Thank you," I say as I weigh its contents;
They feel disproportionately heavy.

"There's going to be a celebration,"
Says Catherine, "To mark my departure.
I'd love it if you were to come along.
I would like to say goodbye properly."

"Of course I'll be there," I tell her, smiling
Even though I do not feel like smiling.
I do not want to say goodbye to her.
I dearly wish that Catherine would stay.

"Until then," she says, turning on her heel.
She returns to her work, and so do I;
Hauling my children's lives through the tall halls,
I search for a quiet place to read them.

Ciara was born almost a month early,
As if she was eager to see the world.
Even in her incubator she squirmed,
Irritated by her small enclosure.

She had the loudest voice in the whole ward,
Letting everyone know she was alive,
And even in her sleep she would burble,
As if she were practising how to speak.

Almost as soon as she learned how to walk
I would lose her; she started exploring
Every inch of our house and beyond it,
Finding creative ways to hide from me.

Everywhere Ciara went, she made a mess;
Toys strewn haphazardly throughout the house,
Mud trampled across the carpets and tiles,
Furniture covered in sticky hand-prints.

She loved drawing with pencils and crayons,
But mere paper was not enough for her.
Unsatisfied by those small canvases,
She drew on the walls, and sometimes herself.

When she was old enough to attend school
I had to spend ages every morning
Brushing the knots tangled into her hair
By all her kinetic activity.

She would return home with pieces of art;
Messy sculptures of mixed materials;
Pipe cleaners, and foam, and papier mâché
Arranged to look a bit like animals.

By the time she was six, we had a zoo
Of bright, glitter-stained, partially feathered
And peculiarly shaped animals
Perched on every available surface.

Slowly, she began to find some focus.
She started with scrap-books, gluing pictures
Cut out from magazines and newspapers,
And doodling across them with her pencils.

Then, she started copying the pictures;
Drawing crude approximations at first,
Before learning how to draw what she saw.
She would spend hours absorbed in her art.

Before I left, she won a prize at school;
A commendation for her artistry.
We pinned the certificate to the fridge,
Surrounded on all sides by her drawings.

Yet, I think it is her zoo I miss most.
All those bright animals placed everywhere,
Filling our house with brilliant colours;
The raw creativity of a child.

Ciara was married when she was eighteen.
In the photographs she still looks so young;
Too small to be wearing such a rich dress,
Ducking to shield herself from confetti.

She and he settled down in Aberdeen.
He worked as a marine biologist
Helping to research ways of repairing
The North Sea's overfished ecosystem.

Ciara taught art at the local college.
There are commendations in her records
From students and colleagues, praising her work;
By all accounts she was much beloved.

Yet she retired young to raise her children,
A girl and a boy, Hayley and Thomas.
From here, Ciara's records start to splinter
Into sub-files about my grandchildren.

Hayley was bright – at the top of her class.
She went on to study mathematics
And from there began a renowned career
Supplementing stellar cartographers.

She was married much later on in life,
To an astronaut often in orbit.
They had only one child, called Emily,
Who grew to have a deep love of painting.

Thomas, meanwhile, grew to be his father;
A marine biologist, researching
The recovering fish population
Filling the North Sea with silvery life.

Thomas was married to two different men.
His first marriage did not last very long,
But his second endured through to his death.
His pictures reveal a long, happy life.

Once both of her children had flown her nest
Ciara returned to teaching for a while,
But she always put her family first,
Spending time with them whenever she could.

They often took family holidays,
Gathered annually at bright beaches,
Warming themselves at log-cabin firesides,
And trekking up perilous mountain paths.

Ciara lived well into her seventies
And was survived by all her family.
They gathered together at her deathbed,
Her husband, her children and her grandchild.

There are pictures of them all together,
And Ciara is smiling, swaddled in sheets,
Surrounded on all sides by real flowers
Dripping vivid petals down her shoulders.

I think Benson was born a collector.
When I first held him, swaddled as he was,
He reached out to grip my silver necklace,
Pudgy fingers curling and uncurling.

Anything near him he would reach out for;
Buttons started to go missing from shirts,
Brooches and pens and errant fallen leaves;
Feeling with his fingers shapes and textures.

By the time he was three he was sorting,
His treasures arranged by his own designs,
Sometimes by colour, sometimes by texture,
Sometimes by the noises made when shaken.

Feathers became his favourite for a while;
He liked the feel of them across his face.
I often saw him chasing after birds,
Hoping to scare a stray feather from them.

When he was old enough to start reading,
He took great pains to arrange his bookshelves.
Sometimes he would order his books by size,
Sometimes by colour, sometimes by genre.

Yet, not long after he started reading,
His collections, which were always so neat,
Started to make a lot less sense to me;
The arrangements he made became obscure.

Sometimes Benson attempted to explain
Why this rock must be placed beside that book;
Why some feathers must be kept separate.
I struggled to follow his reasoning.

His arrangements had become too complex;
Amalgamations of categories;
Strange processes of experiencing
Objects; imposing order upon them.

Yet, his arrangements made him so happy.
Even as I grew apart from Benson,
No longer able to understand him,
His happiness in turn made me happy.

Sometimes, I used to enter my office
To find my books and papers reordered,
And arranged among them would be treasures;
Pebbles, and coins, and feathers, and buttons.

I never reprimanded him for it.
Benson was not an affectionate child,
And his rearrangements of my office
Were his way of telling me he loved me.

Benson began to study medicine
Shortly after graduating from school.
It took him ten long years to qualify
And begin working as a trained doctor.

I picture him striding hospital wards,
Asking patients after their ailments;
Quelling pains and administering cures;
Bringing order to a world without it.

For a while he worked in the villages
Scattered about the remote highland hills,
Officeless and driving from door to door,
Tending to the elderly and infirm.

So far, there has been no mention of love:
No girlfriends or boyfriends in the records,
No marriages, or adoptions, or friends,
And I wonder if my son was lonely.

Eventually he moved through to Glasgow,
There setting himself up in a clinic
And practising general medicine
Until his career suddenly changed.

Benson was offered a prime position
At Glasgow's first euthanasia clinic;
The doctor in charge of patient welfare
And the administration of poison.

I am surprised to see he accepted.
The first patients arrived almost at once,
Begging my son for the relief of death;
A wish that he was empowered to grant.

The bulk of Benson's records are the names
Of the patients whose lives he helped to end.
There are almost endless pages of them
Hundreds and hundreds dead by his needle.

Benson worked for decades at the clinic,
Entire graveyards filled by his steady hand.
There is still no mention of family;
Alone, he ended the lives of thousands.

At last, in his old age, Benson retired,
Returning to one of his rural towns,
And there settling down in a small cottage
Until his terminal diagnosis.

Without any hope of finding a cure,
Benson's life ended in his own clinic
Where he was administered the poison
He used to end so many lives himself.

Observe keenly the young man named Arthur Sigmund
Who has stopped on the moon on his way back to Earth.
This is purely an act of tourism for him,
Stamping the regolith just to see the dust rise,
Making his own footprints among the multitude.
There are queues at the Columbia museum
To see Armstrong's print, preserved in a thick glass box
Where it stands at the foot of the Eagle lander.
The print is a series of miniature craters
Which have made more impact than any meteor.
Yet, Arthur avoids the queues and instead inspects
The replica of the Columbia module;
That small space where the third man waited in orbit
While Armstrong and Aldrin made their lunar landing.
Michael Collins was the first man to be alone,
Truly apart and cut off from humanity
In the time he spent on the far side of the moon.
Defying the guard rails, Arthur mounts the display
To sit where Collins sat all those decades ago.
The replica's hatch is actually functional
And sealing it grants a measure of privacy.
Alone, Arthur contemplates true isolation,
To be cut off, sight and sound, from the distant Earth,
With only a tiny capsule to keep you safe.
Collins reported calm and awe, Arthur has read.
By the time Arthur leaves the module replica
The museum has closed and the lights are switched off.
He wanders the empty hallways, solitary,

Until he comes to a massive set of windows
Beyond which is an expanse of untouched surface
Aglow with the first fleeting moments of Earthrise.
As Arthur watches, the Earth breaks the horizon,
A crescent so bright it streaks across his vision.
From here, it is blue and white and green and so small.
Arthur was expecting the Earth to seem mighty
But instead it appears to be very fragile:
A spherical ornament made of such thin glass
That he could shatter it with a careless gesture.

The *Calypso*'s grand theatre is full.
The crew are crammed together in the stands,
So small beneath the billowing curtains
Drawn across the enormous, gilded stage.

I am surrounded by cheering people
And jostled as they clap and stamp their feet.
Normally I am not claustrophobic,
But I have to fight a strong urge to flee.

Catherine's arrival is a relief.
The crew part for her as she approaches,
Sending ripples through the sea of people
As if all are afraid of touching her.

When she takes her place, sitting beside me,
Our neighbours shuffle warily away,
Leaving a ring of people around us.
She says, "Looks like I arrived just in time."

There is the striking of stringed instruments;
The grandiose blare of the brass section
To the rhythm of thunderous drumming
As the orchestra's performance begins.

In the broad box beneath the stage they sit,
All eyes fixed on their conductor's baton.
With the flick of his wrist, he directs them
Through their bombastic echoing clamour.

As the song begins, the stage curtains part
To reveal the sky above the new world.
This window is the largest I have seen,
Offering an unparalleled vista.

The new world is wreathed in writhing black clouds
Beneath the silver glow of the nanites
Reflecting all the force of the pale sun
Down upon that turbulent remaking.

I sympathise with the seething new world,
Its surface shrouded with violent storms.
Lightning flickers across the blackest clouds,
Tiny bursts of light disrupting the dark.

When those storms clear, the surface will emerge,
Revealing the new world's rivers and seas;
Mountains will rise high around deep valleys,
Snow settling across the tallest peaks.

When my stormy thoughts clear, I will emerge,
A new me, tempered by my children's lives.
My new knowledge whirls around in my head,
An upheaval slowly transforming me.

The orchestra's song rises and rises
As Sigmund finally arrives on stage.
Alone and utterly dwarfed by that sky,
He stands before it and raises his hands.

Rainbow cables are wrapped around his arms,
Leading from his gloved fingers to his feet,
Where they vanish away into the wings.
Sigmund gestures, and the heavens respond.

The nanite clouds billow and whirl about,
Manipulated as if they are paint
And the new world's sky is Sigmund's canvas.
The nanites shimmer silver as they shift.

This performance is a rearrangement,
Fine-tuning the nanites' drift in orbit
To make the surface more than temperate.
Sigmund is giving the new world seasons.

With the turn of his glove, the nanites part
To reveal the sun – a blinding presence
In absolute contrast to the black moons
That still speckle the pale sky like ink drops.

A spinning tunnel of nanites is formed;
A white vortex of light fiercely beaming
Summer upon the southern hemisphere
And brightening the dark moons in between.

The revealed moons turn silver in the light;
Celestial discs mirroring the sun.
Their shadows darken the storm clouds below;
Black circles where there are new eclipses.

Sigmund draws his hands slowly together
And the nanites form a silvery veil,
Dimming the new world's northern hemisphere:
Plunging it into a sudden winter.

Subtler patterns form in the nanite clouds
As Sigmund instructs them with his fingers.
Summer and winter are not quite enough;
The new world's seasons need a gradient.

The nanites gush, forming flowing patterns
That will give the surface spring and autumn.
The tunnel of clouds that circle the sun
Spins with trails and wisps of glittering clouds.

The orchestra reaches a crescendo,
Trembling the theatre with their clamour
As Sigmund clenches both of his raised fists,
Releasing his control over the sky.

The theatre erupts into applause.
Beyond the window the nanite clouds swirl,
Locked now into their seasonal routines.
Sigmund turns to his audience and bows.

The crew stand, stamping their feet and cheering,
Eyes wide with wonder at the new world's sky.
Yet, Catherine and I remain seated;
The only silence in the noisy hall.

Ciara has lived the life I should have lived.
She died surrounded by her family
While flowers dripped their petals all down her;
Real flowers, plucked from the Earth's fertile soil.
All I have here are poor facsimiles:
Green plastic moulded around bent wire frames;
Petals made of a composite fabric
That will never wilt and never decay.
I have such a rage swirling inside me
And I know that I need to release it
Before it can consume me completely,
And make me a danger to the mission.
The object of my anger still orbits;
The probe that brought my children's lives to me.
It has been emptied of information
And would not be missed were it to vanish.
Nobody tries to stop me from stealing
A vacant shuttle, engine left idle.
I am an amateur pilot at best,
But the shuttle's controls are quite simple.
Soaring free of the *Calypso*, I fly,
Searching the nanite clouds for a signal,
Or evidence of the probe's broad orbit;
Subtle eddies disturbing the nanites.
The inertia is enough to press me
Hard against the grey fabric of my seat.
My suit compensates, keeps me comfortable
As the shuttle's engines force me further.

There was a picture of Ciara skiing
With her children down a steep mountain slope,
Their frozen faces fixed in beaming smiles,
Utterly beloved to each other.

The shuttle registers the probe's beacon.
I instruct it to alter our orbit
So that we might arrive alongside it.
My suit whirs as the inertia strengthens.

The shuttle makes a thousand adjustments,
Swinging me violently through the sky
Until our arc is complimentary
To that travelled by the orbiting probe.

It emerges from the nanites flashing,
Red and green lights blinking to herald it,
Beaten solar panel arms still outstretched.
The shuttle's thrusters direct me closer.

When the shuttle settles into orbit
I float free of my seat, gravityless,
Securing my suit's helmet and breathing
Its sterile supply of fresh oxygen.

The shuttle's airlock cycles in seconds
And I am exposed to the vast white sky.
Untethered, I push free of the shuttle.
Alone I fly, crossing the great divide.

The silver nanite clouds gush around me,
Like vapour, they roll harmlessly over,
Sparkling as I plunge through the mass of them.
There, before me, is the probe's silhouette.

My suit's thrusters burst to keep me stable,
Slowing me so that I can land safely.
Grabbing hold of one of the probe's railings,
I lock my magnetic boots to its hull.

Ciara has lived the life I should have lived.
A life devoted to her family,
To seeing them grow up and find success,
Loving them and loved by them each in turn.

Sabotaging the probe is quite simple.
Behind a metal panel are controls;
Its fuel supply is low from its journey,
But there is enough left for one more thrust.

The probe's ancient boosters fire one last time.
I push off before I am dragged along,
Watching as it tumbles into the clouds,
Thrusters burning blue and white with plasma.

The nanites clear enough for me to see
The probe as it enters the atmosphere.
It brightens as white as a signal flare,
Flames engulfing its bent and beaten hull.

Yet, behind it is a more awesome sight.
The new world's storms have started to clear up,
Revealing great, glittering expanses,
Against which the probe is a mere candle.

I am suspended in the sky alone,
In awe of the new world's geography.
It is more gorgeous than I imagined,
Continents revealed across its surface.

The last of the probe burns into nothing,
One last white flash to mark its departure,
Yet I remain floating in the heavens,
Observing the last of the clearing storms.

The new world is now blue and white and grey;
Aglow with all its emerging waters
As they reflect the light of the heavens.
The only colour it still lacks is green.

I, we

the catalyst

our garden heart

brimming full to burst;

we will green the new world

find the cracks in the rocks and rise

our faces turned to our sharpened star, seasons

waxing and waning by the design of their architect;

he, now wearied, stone dry eyes dampened and streaming

as if he wetted and salted the new world's oceans with his tears

he, all our statue symbol, gripping our hands hard enough to mark

promising us remembrance, Sigmund tells us we are beloved

yet his choir remain distant, hesitant to press their touch

to our fertile skin, as if our transcendence is sacred;

they touch us only with their trembling noise

their voices raised harmoniously

as if they might carry me

worldward with

their song

this gathering

marks our departure

tables dripping with foods

recycled through countless bodies

pipes painted to appear Grecian pillars

tapestries waving in the air gushing from vents;

grapes, we think grapes, and force our skin to split

a branching fractal forming from the flesh chasm in our arm

engorging bulbous rich red blood red grapes, we pluck them free

rich and sweet, they are heavy with their cores which we spit
a discord as stones clamour across a mirror chrome saucer
the choir's song clips, falters with their uncertainty
but I am not devouring me, because I am we
chimera and catalyst, multiple and plural
our resemblance is only skin deep
I smooth my skin ravine
and behold she
Rochelle
primitive thing
returned from outside
her useless sabotage complete
anathema now to Sigmund's design
she is crowned queen of great *Calypso*'s exiles
yet redeemed for us; she is, we think, our dear friend
the one we will miss most of all when we are transformed;
newly arrived, we offer her the remainder of our grapes
she takes them gratefully, peeling the red red skin
digging the seeds from the flesh with her nails
hungrily, she devours this offering of us
complimenting the fruit's sweetness
we wish all the best for her
unenhanced: naked,
yet beloved
of us

I wonder again about Catherine;
The way she transformed all those New Terrans,
Converting them into a grand garden.
Was that a genocide, or transcendence?

My son slipped his needle into thousands;
Thousands that gave him consent to do so,
Legally sanctioned by his government.
Should I consider those killings murders?

I dissect Catherine's grapes one by one,
Digging the seeds from the red depths of them.
I know they are juicy and delicious,
But I am unable to enjoy them.

This celebration is too loud for me,
Revellers revelling obnoxiously,
Spilling their pink wines over each other,
Teeth gritty with the seeds of their dull fruits.

The long table reserved for engineers
Is empty except for the three of us,
But the crew lay platters at every chair:
Steaming heaps of food that will go to waste.

The tall chamber quietens for a time
As a figure I recognise orates:
The crew's herald recites some poetry
In the English-esque language of the crew.

Where the verse is composed of words I know,
It becomes apparent that the poem
Is a kind of historical record,
Recounting some of the years while I slept.

The events the herald recites for us
Sound mythological, made colourful
By the lyrical rhythms of the verse.
He tells us of ancient wars and heroes.

I decide that I will find the herald
Once Catherine has left the *Calypso*,
And ask him about the awakening:
Why only us three engineers remain.

The herald's recital lasts for hours,
A wearying soporific poem
Lulling us all to sleep with its rhythm.
Even the herald's eyes begin to droop.

When at last the poem comes to an end
The bright hall is hushed as many slumber.
Sigmund's chin rests on his chest – he dozes.
Only Catherine seems to be alert.

Taking my hand, she leads me from the hall
And through the *Calypso*'s arched corridors,
The fresh air rousing me from the rhythms
Of the herald's mixed-language recital.

Catherine takes me to the colonists,
The huge chamber where they slumber in sacs,
Human silhouettes encased in amber
That has a fleshy warmth and skin texture.

There are thousands of colonists in here,
All presented to me in rows and racks
As if they are corpses in body bags;
I can't seem to shake Benson from my thoughts.

"It's nearly time for you to start your work,"
Catherine tells me. "You have to be strong.
The future of the new world's colony
Depends on the strength of your conviction."

I do not feel particularly strong.
I search myself and find uncertainty.
"I don't want you to go," I say to her.
"I can't stand up to Sigmund by myself."

There is a small porthole window nearby,
Beyond which turns the glinting blue new world.
Catherine takes me to it and gestures,
The sweep of her hand encompassing all.

"If you ever need me, just look outside,
Or fly down and walk among my forests.
Remember that this isn't death, Rochelle.
This is my final metamorphosis."

"Still," I say. "I am going to miss you."
When I embrace her she is strangely soft,
As if she might burst if I squeeze too tight.
My vision blurs as my eyes fill with tears.

We remain there, stood beside the porthole,
Beneath the racks filled with the colonists
Until it is time for her to depart.
She is escorted away by the crew.

Catherine takes one last glance back at me,
Her kaleidoscopic eyes glistening.
Where her tears fall, tiny flowers blossom,
Each droplet bursting into sudden life.

FOUR

think

of a child

born too small

its tiny heart trembling

skin so thin its veins are visible

a red, wrinkled thing helpless and dying

needled and cocooned, we were saved; augmented,

our fluttering mothwing heart given blue whale strength

so that our blood became ocean blood, washing waves through us;

when we grew up, we felt the moon's tidal tug in our veins

we waxed and waned with dear Luna's seasons

our ocean blood dually pulled by her orbit

and influenced by her silver glow,

our heart still remembering

its mothwing flutter;

our marrow

was made sap

a sickly golden syrup

giving our bones bough strength,

so that no part of us might ever be snapped;

our knuckles and knees were the knots of trees and

we would often stand with our feet buried in the soft earth

spreading our toes like burrowing roots, wrists bared up to the sun;

we felt the earth's seasons run deep through our sap marrow,

every winter hibernating, lulled always by the frosty chill,

and every spring blushing the colours of blossom;

each year added a ring to our bough bones,

increasing our wood forest fortitude

until we became not a tree

but a grove entire;

our eyes

were enhanced

to falconic sharpness

and augmented further still;

inspired by the senses of migrating birds

we too can feel magnetic fields: they emerge in sight

as strict silvery threads, netted across the domed whirl of the sky,

and they tingle the tips of our fingers should we close our proximity,

as if we too might know them through our feathers while in flight;

we can also see some radiations: a shimmering misty haze

and ultraviolet light, making the faces of flowers neon

and the wings of insects deliciously bright;

we would gaze often at beetle shells,

their refractive carapaces

an endless delight;

I, us, we

the chimera

a child born sickly

and in every way improved

year by year enhanced ever further

breaking every boundary in bioengineering

eradicating all our raw inherited human weaknesses

to become this, us, something not human but better than human

a person, or persons, and an ocean, and a forest, and all the birds in the sky

engineered to a final brilliant purpose: this, now, our transcendence;

we will burst and become truly plural at last, our multiple selves

unravelling and catalysing not a child but a whole world;

through ribbon arcs of magnetic fields we descend

our ocean blood gushing, our sap marrow hot,

all our senses indulged by the sky

and the new world's moons

which tug at us

as we fall

we observe

the great *Calypso*;

she, a hollow moon turning

her core a dark pricked with stars,

and we remember every *Calypso* that was:

she, a thin frame composed of towed scaffolding,

a sketched circle aglitter with construction crew thrusters;

she, a dream, a suggestion, a manifesto, a blueprint made manifest,

all of her as chimeric as we are; each arch an arc of Martian ore forged,

her fuels compounds made of meteors and asteroids and comets,

her organic elements descendants of Earth's ancient growths,

we will miss walking her too-tall echoing halls;

we watch the great *Calypso* diminish

glowing in twin sickles of light

as she orbits sunward;

dear circlet,

goodbye

we plummet

our shuttle rattling

with micrometeor impacts

that sound like hailstones bouncing;

we pass the meteor field and there before us

darkly aglitter is New Terra, shrouded in nanite clouds;

New Terra brightens with the sparking engines of missile launches,

each a tiny aggression billowing into a useless flower explosion

lacking the strength to scratch our shuttle's bulkheads;

we fly too fast, barely shaken by the rockets

until we are free of that moon's grip

and there wholly before us

is the new world

its surface

bright

welcoming

the new world is

a lidless eye always open

drawing us closer with its mass

daring us to plunge deep into its ocean iris;

the atmosphere distorts the stars at its dark horizon

as if each point of light is falling from the edge of the world;

our shuttle rattles as we chase those spilling stars, flying towards night;

this, we know, is our last glimpse of the new world from on high

so we etch the fissures of its barren plates across our skin

tracing peaks and troughs for mountains and valleys

as if we might somehow scar it into ourselves;

we become a mirror, reflecting seas,

remembering continents

in our very flesh

then, we fall

dragged

from orbit

bulkheads bright

nose cone flaring white

into the atmosphere, burning;

we are a star streaking through the sky

making a wish upon ourselves, arms crossed

the blue blue depths rushing too quick up to meet us;

it feels as if we must fall through the sky and sea and deeper

down through the crust and mantle and to the very core of the world

where we will become molten; our fore-thrusters fire at last

rippling the suddenly too-close waves of the ocean

yet we plunge through that frantic surface

shocked and jarred by the impact

darkness enveloping us

before we rise

floating

our lander

hissing steam

and bobbing on waves

we uncross our arms and stand

unlatching the rooftop hatch to climb

free of the shuttle, we take our first deep breath

tasting the new world's delicious sky, gulping fresh air

below is blue and above is blue but for wisps of white clouds

we unskin ourselves from our suit, enjoying the slow undressing

as we bear ourselves fully to the new world, feeling the wind,

the flecks of sea spray that splash across our naked toes,

we expose ourselves tenderly, proudly like a lover,

stowing all our discarded articles back below

we set the shuttle's controls and rise,

sealing the hatch beneath us

we stretch our arms

and dive clear

chilled

by the sea

those great depths

distant beneath us, we rise

floating upon the waves to watch

our shuttle as it climbs on bursts of blue fire

rocking us with the power of its ascent, a bright spark

streaking into the blue until it becomes a gleaming star flaring

we are alone at last, all entire ourselves with no cumbersome wrappings

exposed utterly to the sea, we are content to float a while longer;

up there, so high, is the silhouette of a ring: the *Calypso*

casting her circular shadow across the low waves

we wait until the shuttle's gleam is gone

then fill our lungs to bursting

as if we might inhale

all the sky

we dive down

all our selves immersed

bubbles rising from our mouth

until we split our skin into slashes, gills
so that the new world's ocean rushes through us
the brine thick across our tongue as we breathe water
webbing film across our fingers and our toes and our eyes
kicking deeper towards the black depths where no light reaches
feeling the weight of all that water upon us, the pressure pushing at us
until daylight is but a distant glimmer and we are alone in the vast deepness
forcing glows from the tips of our fingers, we watch those seeds shimmer
little pale blue lanterns wriggling, squirming, seeking each other
we go deeper still, trailing twinkling seeds with our toes
they twitch, all pale, a bloom of writhing lights
they themselves splitting, multiplying
until the ocean is a night sky
filled with living stars
we kick deep down
to the cracks and chasms
still rumbling beneath the new sea
among plumes of dust we swim; they gush
from seething vents spewing their violent warmth
the ground flashing with fleeting ruptures of seething lava
the ocean floor made and remade with raw vivid molten stone
here, we shimmer more seeds from ourselves and watch them catalyse
the heat rippling them as they form and divide, whirling like carousel lights
gripping hold of the hot cracked rocks they take root, worming upwards
tendrils flickering in the heat, a deep garden spreads out beneath us
into fungus-like shapes the seeds bloom; billowing in fractals
we diminish as we do this, force these sudden growths,
so we only give the essential amount of ourselves;
enough that this seething colony manifests
sustainably exploding itself outwards
we see the deep garden unfurl
spreading in the hot dark
in every direction;
we kick up

towards light

feeling the currents

swimming among our seeds

some of which now see with eyes;

proto-fish-things gush silvery all around

finding their first forms, testing tentacles and tails

the catalysing process skipping natural selection altogether

we turn in their midst, swarmed by jellyfish glows, globular shapes,

seeing them spread out in every direction as if they might fill the whole sea

which they will, we know, given days and months and years; we rise higher still

following the flow of water through the ocean, letting ourselves be pulled

to where white slivers of daylight pierce the depths and illuminate us,

make aglow the scales of the living things finding their shapes

and we dearly hope that there will be whales, above all else:

whales to fill these new oceans with music, with songs;

we rise up enough to see the high waves above

there is wind, a storm, lightning flashing

and ahead there is an island shape

a splinter risen from low

we kick across

and emerge

from the waters

onto a prickle of rocks

still sharp-edged from upheaval

our back spattered with the spray of waves

our face upheld to the grey sky darkly raining down

all is soaked, all glistens in the pale sunlight leaking through

the island rises ahead of us, a shard of land thrust up with colossal force

its jagged peak struck by lightning again and again, splintering that risen stone

we fill ourselves with the damp air, breath snatched by the whirling gale

clambering quadrupedally inland, we wish for a tail for balance;

rocks slide around us, clattering, spun by the wild weather

these fringes will one day be beaches, we think;

these boulders will be jutting cliffs, eroded,

overseeing dunes, pebbles and sand

while warped trees cling hold

their roots buried deep

in rocky fissures

we pause

inside a cave

a shallow dry crack

too young for stalactites

we watch the white waves below

crashing and flinging glinting flecks high

here, we can hear the island growling a low rumble;

we scrape our hands across the jagged walls, feel it tremble,

crumble the dark matter between our fingers, all soft, charcoal-like

we follow the trail of scorched substance through the cave, feeling its route

until we emerge fully into an open field, made squelching, muddy by the tempest;

this broad valley between shatter-shard rises is a basin, through which a rough river flows

wetting the dark matter which we kneel within, spreading our fingers and toes;

it is a lot like compost, so gorgeously rich with minerals and nutrients

it feels as if it might explode into sudden new life unprovoked

yet, without us, we know all this would remain inert;

we go across to the river, that murky stream,

watching the rain ripple the flow

then we spread our arms

and burst wide

life radiates from us

our chest our stomach hot

our arms and legs flushed through

our vision whirling, we feel fierce vertigo

feel ourselves fray at the edges and come apart

all our internals made external, we catalyse the island

the river blooms green and purple, flecks caught up in the wind

around our feet grasses rise, slicing our skin, drawing our fertile blood

which blossoms into flowers around us, winding themselves around our ankles

trees gushing upwards gushing towards the sky so quick they twist, crackle and creak

all that was dark and cold and wet now green but not just green, white and yellow and red
so much sudden colour inside us and outside us, we feel our skinny ribs shuddering
our thoughts a blurred hot delirium, we let ourselves disintegrate a little more
not too much just enough just enough for crawling things that drip from us
droplets shivering like sweat, splashing into worm shapes that burrow
finding their lengths, finding their skins that ooze across them
worms that writhe among the roots, maggots that wriggle
peeling themselves from their pupae so quick
unfurling their new wings, they fly
buzz up and whirl in a haze
there must be swarms;
turning our wrists
we hive them
hexagonal fractures
forming across our skin
where new larvae bulge white
before they rip quick, insects emerging
all pollinators, all queens, wasps, bees and ants
sudden butterflies and moths billowing their bright wings
the insect hum now so thick it vibrates through the depths of our bones
enough, this is enough now, we clench our fists and teeth and our hives crumble
and we tumble among the rich roots now strengthless, gulping lungfuls of air and river;
throes of delirium sweep through us, winged and unwinged things crawl across us
but nothing decays; the thick hot forest surrounding us remains fixed and alive
swaying in the storm and still finding its form, the new trees bear fruit
bulging from their branches are sudden engorged heavy shapes
gnawed at by insects and us, biting juicy tonguefuls
the fruits are segmented and sour and sweet
we rest a while, eating and cooling
restoring our drained strength
before rising renewed
we follow the river
parting trees
the fissure winds

to the base of a high hill;

a shard rising tall from the ground

we clamber up the cut sharp splinter rocks

which open our skin, weeping our blood which rolls

forming trees that cling to outcrops, roots among the fractures

the higher we climb, the stronger the winds that buffet us, threatening

to throw us from these heights, to tumble us back to the forming forest below

yet we grip hold tight, force ourselves upright, until we reach the cracked shard peak

the storm whirls around us as we brace our bloodied feet and open our arms

to a sheltered fracture, rolling beads from our palms that thicken white

some speckled, others clean, the eggs engorge and split wide

shells broken by new beaks, dark eyes peering high

they shrug their prisons from their feathers

totter to the cliff edge on their claws

spread their new wings open

caught on the wind

they soar

only tiny birds

for this small island

but enough to breed, thrive

we stumble back among the wings

crunching across the cracked rocks down

where we descend, the island garden follows

all is green behind us, all ahead still forming itself;

the process now inevitable without us, we stride the hills

until we find a series of cave-like cracks where roots writhe;

there, we go to our knees, grip the new grasses and open our throat;

those fruits we swallowed now transformed inside ourselves, they emerge:

rolling small bodies with tails that wriggle, they uncurl and grow fur and claws

rodents bare their new teeth and breathe and skitter into the dark cracks

gnawing at roots at insects at each other, they screech and scuttle

flowing from our mouth until we are empty of them all

we wait a while, exhausted through, sucking air

surrounded by the alive island, loud now

with all the life we have given it
we stumble slow beyond
from forest to shore
to the waves
which lick high
cascading droplets
over our wearied ankles
we are smaller than we were
lighter, weaker, for this island's life
the storm swirls and we long for stillness
for the line of bright blue visible at the horizon
we dive, dragging brine through our throat-slit gills
discovering that the depths are now teeming with new life
schools that sweep in silver slivers, arcing beneath us and around us
we swim through a fluther of jellyfish undulating their neon brightnesses
prickled by their electric presences, we ripple them as we kick past
enveloped by silvery fishes, we glide through their slick scales
to where pillars of daylight illuminate grey shells and fins
some tinged green, some tinged red, some tinged blue
the turtles glide, eyes turned to the breaking sky
while beneath us, shadowy things swim;
announced only by their presences
proto-whales meander the deep
the water warms around us
as we leave the storm
for open skies
above us now, blue
each wave a brief prism
refracting the light of the sun
we rise to the surface, resting there
our skin warming, breath slowing, we go
floating further still from the distant black storm
until, beneath us, shard shelves rise, shallowing the depths,
expanses of stone forming shattered plates where smaller fish dart

their scales and tails glittering silver as they sliver from crack to crack;

we remain afloat, but let ourselves relax so fully, so completely, that we dissolve;

the edges of us disperse into this shallow place, each exhalation scattering more of us

until from the warm rocks arise skeletal shapes, bristling plates, plumes of tubes;

life in such seething abundance that not a gap remains; all here is enmeshed;

the tallest fractal structures reach hand-like to touch our exposed back

and we think that it would be so easy to stay here and be the reef,

to dissolve completely across these heated rock plates

and become the corals and weeds and starfish,

but there is still much for us to do ahead;

we dive down to the coral plates

and see what writhes there;

slick eels oozing curling

around cracks and corals;

we worm with them, swimming

through weeds heavy with red pods

already ready to disperse themselves further,

past shelves encrusted with barnacles and limpets

their corrugated shells ruddy, pock-marked and sun-hot

to where long-jawed fish snap at coral retreats and rocky cracks

where tiny fishes in all colours convalesce, safe in their living complexes;

all at once, a shadow passes overhead: not a cloud, but a moon casting its eclipse,

the reef darkens but in the new gloom is neon; the arms of star-fish luminous

among striped coral plates ribbed with glowing green and yellow nubs;

lightning blue courses across the backs of the meandering eels

and the hearts of tiny fish are visible through their scales,

red blood aglow as it courses richly through them;

the eclipse is brief, confusing the new life,

sunlight gushing again in moments,

obliterating all the glows;

the reef will adapt

given time

the moons' arcs

will be commonplace

each eclipse not a miracle,

just the swing of an astral pendulum;

three moons crowd the open sky right now

crescents so slender that they are bright incisions

dividing blue from blue; even here we can feel them tug

their competing gravities making them dance across the heavens;

diminished and weary, we push away from the reef even as it still unfurls;

we are smaller now, smaller than we were, but still enough for what is to come;

the shallows shallow, making mirror pools of the water between sharp blade shards

rocks like razors leaving red lines across us from which writhe slick leeches

spiral teeth latch and hungry bodies bulge; we are sucked at every angle

our rich blood leaking inky crimson and black through the waters

the ink by which this damp humid heated place will be writ;

the gorged leeches overeat themselves into ripeness

writhing deliriously away before they burst

spraying red black tear droplets

which seed the rich mulch

spiralling into reeds

and new trees

branches billow

trunks twisting; bent

heavy-backed trees heave

deep green leaves gasping for light;

at a mulch shore, we stand among the reeds

tugging the last of the leeches from our torn flesh

we let ourselves bloody the swamp as we rise and stride

crimson droplets dividing into frogspawn jellies like oversize cells

from which wriggle tadpoles, growing leaping legs, oily skin in quicktime

frogs and toads and skinks and newts bubble the churning pools of the swamp

hungry amphibious things sliding from wet to dry to wet among the reeds

our blood rolls from our shoulders and fizzes into insects at our palms

mosquitoes spear us with their probing proboscises, supping us

tiny bellies bulging red, they gorge themselves into bursting

spraying the air with shimmering flies and beetles

amphibious tongues leaping at the thick air

snatching tiny bodies, the frogs crunch;

we go deeper, our blood sopping;

tiny vermillion birds whir

from our belly flesh

humming wings

so noisy

at a clear lake

we stumble and kneel

blood rolling from our tongue

we heave our dark innards outwards

jewelled snakes sliding from our open throat

rippling in the crystal waters as they slither hither

our ribs are wracked as we empty ourselves swampward

gobbets of blood crackling into crocodile shapes; they splash

ridged scales piercing the warm waters, slit eyes like the crescent moons

with one last heartsore heave we spit black blood, manifesting wading birds;

some are quick to take flight: tall legs fold beneath broad wings and long beaks

while others are snatched by crocodiles, new bodies smashed and shattered;

we too are feeling smashed and shattered, resting against a weeping tree

admiring the jagged ragged pale peaks that rise beyond the swamp;

those new mountains in the distance already snow speckled

where we will stumble soon and find our final cradle;

for now, we rest and cease to bleed: we breathe

the air so thick with insects we inhale them

feel them buzzing between our cheeks

there is not much left of us now

thin bones and pale flesh

skeletal, we stand

wade wearily onward

through shallower puddles

to where there are no pools at all

a dry place waits beyond the swampland

where the risen continent bakes in the sun's heat

we stride the plain mountainward, those peaks wavering
our vision distorted by the sun's power reflected off the hot rocks
the heat courses across us, brightness burning our exposed flesh, limbs red
our skin peels from us in translucent threaded ribbons: we shed our outermost layers
that skin writhing into serpentine shapes that sidewind across the dusty rocks
crackling into lizards with jewelled armour scales that bathe in the heat
prickling into cacti that rise from the cracks, white spines agleam
we pull the loose skin from our wrists and spin it into spiders
arachnid shapes scuttling and burrowing into the shade
scorpions arching their tails, raising their claws
to herald us as we pass through this place
I, us, we, the oasis, seeding life
even in this barren land
our shedding skin
catalyses
we carry on
to a broad basin
where threaded streams
trickle through the rock cracks;
above the distant peaks, storms whirl
drenching the slopes and forming waterfalls
those falls coalescing into long rivers that run here
soaking the rich soils; in time this will be a lake, we imagine
but for now it will be something other; we tug at strands of our hair
plucking errant threads from our scalp and weaving them, letting them drift
across the damp rocks they gust and where they go grasses spear upright
sharp emerald green blades as tall as trees thrust high at the blue sky
until we are completely surrounded and crunching through grass
unable to see the mountains for the deep plain we have made
from our eyes we pluck lashes and blow them like kisses
those lashes tumbling and trembling in the streams
until they form quadrupedal mammalian shapes
those proto-horses trembling on fawn feet
their triumphant whinnying echoing

as they rear, stamp and canter

trampling green blades

we advance through

unsteadily until

at long last

we arrive

at the shadow

of a shard mountain

the sun ablaze at its peak

as if it has been speared upon it

those pale heights wreathed in mists

blanketed in snow that gleams and drips

melting into reflective waterfalls that gush gold

as if the sun is a fruit, pierced and leaking amber juice

those falls tumbling down the heights, pooling on plateaus

forming streams and rivers that criss-cross the jagged foothills;

we stumble steadily onward, clambering ragged across the torn ground

until the sun is overhead and blazing white, steaming the rivers that surround us

all that water roaring as it gushes past, spraying us with its turbulent flows

here and there we crouch and breathe our breath into damp cracks

making mossy and slippery the glistening shattered rocks;

at a lattice of streams we plunge our skinny arm deep

so that pink and black fishes sliver from our skin

those fishes wriggle, flow like the waters

and we wade, chilled, beyond them

navigating through rainbows

until we emerge, cold

from a still pool

confronted

by a calm place

a cracked convergence

of gentler rock plates like hills

enriched thickly with an earthy mush

which crumbles like cake when we crush it

the rivers here meandering through curved rivulets;
here, we know: here is the cradle place we have been seeking
so tired, we crawl the hills, and where we go the fertile earth blooms
tiny grasses and flowers and trees sprout in a winding snail trail, billowing;
we drag ourselves onwards, up, and wriggling things emerge from our open pores
worms pour from us, and slugs ooze from us, and beetles drip from us
until we writhe with snail-shell curls and carapace shimmers
enriching further the newly enriched soil, we vomit then
gouts of yellow and purple that splatter fungus
tiered mushrooms and plates rise neon
scattering mycelium spores, a haze
settling in spider-web strings;
forming a new network
above and beneath
the black earth
and it is here
upon this hilltop
that we finally collapse
unable to drag ourselves further
we lie with our face to the sky and see
the silhouettes of birds wheeling in the blue;
we indulge all our crude human senses one last time
feeling the sunlight across our skin, the soil beneath our back,
watching the trees slowly rise around us, coiled with fungus blooms,
we taste the rich fertile air, inhale and exhale spores and seeds and insects
all of this is us; our plurality realised so utterly that we weep for joy
our tears becoming tiny birds with long beaks that flit about us
we sigh a long sigh, as if we might exhale all that we were
and with the last of our strength reach for our ribs
take grip of those hard nubs beneath our skin
and pull our chest wide open, revealing
all our innards splayed painlessly;
we let our weary arms drop
our skin unravelling

organs writing

we begin

our

bloom;

seeds

flutter

we are

the head

of a dandelion

blown

the winds

disintegrated

converge here

gusting

and scattering

tumbling

sowing us

our seed selves

our innards drifting

emptying us

fluttering

our organs ceasing

like butterflies

their human functions

like petals

in wisps

we inhale

like smoke

the seething wind

like vapour

until

our lungs

thickening

burst

slowly,

we transform

our body both

larvae

and pupae

until

we feel

our heart

stop

yet

we live

even as we

disintegrate

feeling

ourselves

unfurl

as our
senses   fail   we feel   instead

with the
roots
and
of the trees
the
mycelial

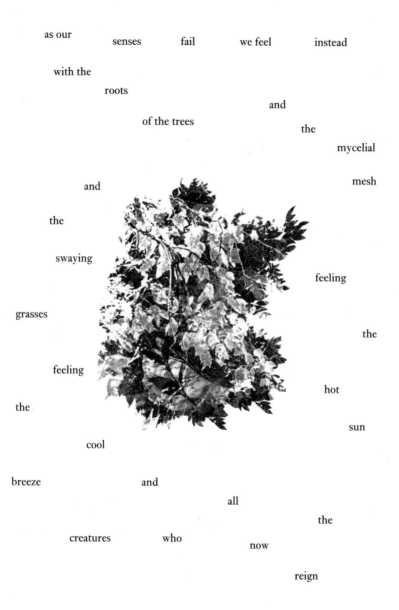

and
mesh

the

swaying
feeling

grasses
the

feeling
hot

the
sun

cool

breeze   and
all
the
creatures   who
now
reign

strange

how

sap-slow

our

thoughts

FIVE

When I was seven, I saw a cartoon
About a group of kids with a secret:
A magical hidden wizard's garden
Where, each week, they had a new adventure.

That cartoon stuck with me for years after,
Not for its predictable storylines
But for the vividness of the wildlife.
I wanted my own enchanted garden.

Nowhere lived up to my expectations;
The grasses were never quite green enough,
The flowers always desaturated,
The humming of the bees a bit too coarse.

To this day, I'm certain I still believe
That rivers should be blue, trees should be brown
The sun circled with yellow triangles;
That all days should have an autumnal warmth.

The *Calypso*'s algae farms are humid;
Beads of moisture drip down the wet-slick walls;
My clothes cling to me here, so drenched in sweat,
Yet I stay, and watch the algae baths swirl.

Catwalks overlook the cylinder vats
Where the crew stir the algae – a green mulch
Thriving beneath ultraviolet lamps,
Shifting strangely in the ship's gravity.

When the heat becomes intolerable
I move through an airlock, take gulping breaths
In the sudden chill of the corridor.
Shivering, I wring out my sodden clothes.

There is an enormous porthole window
And I stand before it, drying my hair,
Watching the new world – a shining blue bead
Surrounded with white and now stained with green.

I find it difficult to reconcile
The mossy growth clinging to the new world
With Catherine, my friend the engineer,
Who I first saw dancing with deep green vines.

Unsettled, I move through the *Calypso*,
Wandering past her manufactories
To her engines – her plasma reactors;
Mostly dormant now we are in orbit.

Colossal conductive metal banks rise,
Surrounding me, humming with potential;
The power to move a ship between stars.
My skin prickles with tiny static bursts.

There is a snap like the crack of a whip
And a flash of light bright enough to scar
A jagged white line across my vision
As a bank discharges its potential.

At the second discharge I realise
My mistake: these engines are not dormant.
Feeling my hair rise up from my shoulders,
I crouch in an attempt to ground myself.

White strikes arc overhead, burning the air,
Each snapping loud enough to tremble me.
I clasp my hands and offer feeble prayer;
This would be a foolish way to perish.

A figure dressed in a strange wire mesh cage
Advances on me, illuminated
As the reactors strike it fiercely.
It shields me as it ushers me forward.

The heat is far worse than the algae farms.
As I traverse the angry corridors
I realise how deep I had wandered,
Unthinking among the ship's plasma banks.

At last I emerge, drenched in sweat again,
Breathing hard of air that is not burning.
The crew converge, their expressions fierce,
Shouting at me in their evolved English.

The mesh suit is glowing, almost molten;
The figure inside waits for it to cool
Before untwisting the melted wire mesh
And revealing a man I recognise.

The herald steps wearily from his suit.
Wiping at his face with a towel, he smiles,
Waving a charred and blackened glove at me.
"Thank you," I tell him, over the crew's shouts.

When the last of the ruined suit is gone,
The herald sits and sips at cool water.
The rest of the crew begin to disperse,
So I sit down next to him, still shaking.

When the worst of the shivering subsides,
I turn to the herald. "Thank you," I say,
"I wasn't thinking. I've been… distracted.
I thought the engines would still be dormant."

"Not yet," the herald tells me, his voice hoarse,
"Sweet *Calypso* still has one journey left."
The crackling plasma banks start to settle,
Dimming the engine's arched antechamber.

Even with my thoughts so muddled, I know
That the *Calypso* has no more journeys;
We are at our final destination.
Confused, I say as much to the herald.

The tall herald shrugs his skinny shoulders.
"I know not where we must go next," he says,
"But Sigmund has ordered us to prepare.
You may question him. It is your purpose."

"I can barely remember my purpose,"
I tell him, "But I will question Sigmund.
First, though, I've been meaning to track you down.
There's something important I need to know."

The herald stands, and then bows before me.
When he kneels, his joints crackle like branches,
Thin bones protruding beneath his thin skin.
"Ask of me what you will," he says, smiling.

"When I woke up, I was alone," I say.
"All the other engineers were missing,
And I was in a kind of quarantine,
Cut off from the rest of the *Calypso*."

The herald nods slowly, seriously.
"I can tell you why, but it will take time,"
He says. "Perhaps a day and maybe more.
Have you time to spare for the tale's telling?"

From what I know, I still have a small while
Before the colonists are awoken
And delivered to the new world's surface.
"Can you give me the short version?" I ask.

The herald seems somewhat disappointed,
But nods gracefully nonetheless. He stands,
Drawing himself up, eyes unfocusing
As he begins to recite his poem.

The expanse a vibrant void bejewelled
Aglitter with radiant stars afire
Was sweet *Calypso*'s celestial sea
Bright with heavenly beacons to guide her
So small she spun in interstellar space
Traversing the deep expanse for ages
While within her walls generations lived
Maintaining her course for that distant sun
Where turned the barren new world awaiting
Calypso's verdant cargo so potent.
The crew: their home the *Calypso*'s archways
Brightened her halls with timeless songs of Earth
Singing joyfully of their ancestors;
Watching so keenly the slumbering saints
Interred and deathless in sarcophagi,
Their vigil a vigil of patient love.
And though their clocks ticked to Terra's rhythms
The *Calypso*'s crew lived to their own time,
Etched into her bulkheads at intervals,
Determined by the slowly changing stars;
A map of time passed in the vast expanse
Surfing waves of light sent from distant suns.
Sometimes a milestone in space would be reached;
So many light-years traversed or so forth,
Necessitating a welcome party
To celebrate her continued success.
Our story begins at one such event:
The fiftieth light-year travelled from Earth,

A miraculous day on her journey,
And one joyfully recounted by all.
The crew's leader then was a king named George
Who needed no crown for he was much loved,
His memory deep and leadership great,
Dressed ever in the crew's simple clothing
As if he were just another of them.
By his command the entire crew gathered
From all corners of the great *Calypso*.
Each section of her had its own faction,
A dynasty built of generations
United beneath heads of families;
Yet still they came, numbered by the thousand,
To celebrate all together for once
This most hallowed and esteemed of milestones.
George commanded splendid decoration
Of the most sacred chamber on the ship;
The mighty hall where Sigmund lay sleeping
Locked in his most regal sarcophagus.
From the balconies flowed golden streamers
Like slivers of sunshine upon his tomb
While the walls were painted in Earthly hues
With hills and forests and long horizons
Worthy of our mission's esteemed leader.
And each faction brought their own offering
The mechanics installed bright projectors
Throwing moving clouds across the arches
As if Sigmund slumbered beneath a sky;
The fabricators brought wreaths of flowers
Artificially made but resplendent
To lay at Sigmund's feet as if he slept
Not in a star-ship but a rich meadow;
The surgeons brought pills filled with memories
Of excellent holidays spent on Earth

So that some of the crew could remember,
In Sigmund's honour, their ancestral home,
Filling his sacred chamber with laughter;
The reclamists brought the bones of dead kings,
Tiny remnants of the crew's dead leaders
To honour Sigmund with their presences,
Each of them a conduit of his will;
The couriers brought their brightest sun-bulbs
To fill every corner of the chamber
With brilliant, white, radiant star-shine,
Banishing the dark from Sigmund's chamber;
The chamberlains brought a gorgeous banquet,
Practising their most Earth-like recipes
So that Sigmund's chamber smelled delicious,
A million mouths watering at once
For those tantalising Earthly flavours;
The artisans scoured the archives for songs
And brought splendid Terran tunes to echo
Across Sigmund's chamber, provoking songs
Sung harmoniously by all present;
The teachers told their finest of stories,
Invoking ancient muses to aid them
In recounting of Earth's greatest tales,
With Sigmund's exploits foremost among them;
The navigators brought maps of the stars
Depicting the *Calypso*'s great voyage,
From her inception at distant Terra
To her destination, still far away,
And her current location, between suns,
The elegant arc of her steady route
Now an entire fifty light-years in length;
More factions arrived and each one in turn
Provided their own great contribution
To king George's splendid celebration,

Every new gift honouring dear Sigmund
And all those engineers who slept elsewhere,
Their lives suspended in sarcophagi
Awaiting the *Calypso*'s arrival
To wake and realise Sigmund's vision
Of a pristine new world, untouched by Earth.
Yet, one faction provided no presents,
Present only in presence, they saw all
With impassive and endless scrutiny.
The custodians did not celebrate,
Instead, they fulfilled their hallowed duty
As guardians, watching over Sigmund
And the rest of the sleeping engineers
With a most stern and fervent vigilance,
Unfaltering over generations.
The captain of the custodians watched
With greater zeal than any of the rest,
Brushing golden streamers from Sigmund's tomb,
Her post at his side, most trusted of all
To protect him from any kind of harm.
Her name was Rochelle, as was tradition;
Each captain named after the engineer
They were originally assigned to;
She was the fourth Rochelle captain named so,
And had taken pride in her assignment,
Researching her slumbering engineer
And learning all their was to know of her.
Rochelle's singular zeal brought her renown,
Enough that she rose quickly through the ranks,
Making captain of the custodians
While still young enough to carry a sword;
Yet, though Rochelle now watched over Sigmund
She never forgot about her namesake,
All she had learned about the engineer

Strengthening her resolve and righteousness,
For it was that engineer's sacred role
To question Sigmund's vision, find its faults
And in that way help him to improve it.
The celebration began in earnest
With factions intermingling liberally
As they had not done in many a year,
Freely dancing and singing and speaking,
And all the while golden streamers showered
And bright lights dazzled, and clouds moved above,
Sigmund's chamber almost bursting with joy;
And George, their leader: he danced among them,
Smiling with old friends and friends newly made,
Bowing his crownless head to each faction
As if he were their servant, not their king,
Before resting at the banquet table
Upon a simple chair made of metal
Not at all suitable to his station;
George feasted then, eating of Earthly foods
And delighting in the craft of them all,
So lovingly constructed, delicious
And reminiscent of his distant home.
Gradually, and over many hours,
A quiet descended on the chamber,
Making way for softer celebration
In the form of sombre song and stories
Shared by the *Calypso*'s best orators,
Entertaining a sated and tired crew;
Only the custodians remained stern,
Statuesque and vigilant at their posts
Watching over Sigmund's sarcophagus
Just as they had done for generations.
Eventually, when all stories were told,
A million pairs of eyes turned to George,

Still sat upon his common metal chair;
It was expected he would make a speech
To end the day's exhausting partying.
So spake king George, his eye upon the crew:
"None of us will live to see the new world.
It is for us to live and die right here,
In this vessel, which we have made our home,
Brightening it with our laughter and songs.
When Sigmund wakes he will make the new world,
But I contend that we have made our own,
Here, beneath the *Calypso*'s great archways;
Our world is a star-ship between the stars;
Our world is its corridors and alcoves;
Our world is pipes and bulkheads and windows;
Our world is our memories and beliefs;
Our world is our tradition and patience;
Our world is diligence and oversight;
Our world is this crew, each other, always.
Each of us has demonstrated today
The very best of what our world can be;
A place where we remember who we are,
Where we have come from, and where we go next;
One day, our descendants will awaken
To the sight of the new world beneath them,
And it will be their most sacred honour
To care for it, guard it, watch over it,
Just as we do for the *Calypso* now.
The new world will be a new paradise,
But I tell you now, my beloved crew,
That we have already made paradise,
Here, on the *Calypso*, with each other."
A long silence fell after George's speech,
Followed, at last, by rapturous applause,
The crew stood and stamped their feet and cheered loud,

Reverberating from the tall archways.
Only the custodians did not cheer,
Remaining wholly stoic, impassive
And apparently unmoved by the speech.
Gradually, as the cheering subsided,
The crew began to disperse for the night,
With the dimming of the courier's bulbs
Lending Sigmund's sarcophagus chamber
An evening air; a moon rose above,
Projected against a starry backdrop,
Illuminating the emptying hall.
Some remained, choosing to sleep in small camps,
While others located nearby alcoves,
Choosing to journey homewards tomorrow
Instead of making the long trip tonight.
And when all was peaceful in the chamber,
Captain Rochelle sent out quiet whispers;
Murmurs spread among the custodians
Of a meeting to occur that same night
In secret, and not in Sigmund's chamber,
But in the halls of the sarcophagi
Where the rest of the engineers slumbered,
Watched over by zealous custodians.
The whispers found the ears of all present
And all the custodians slipped away
But for two left to watch over Sigmund.
Drawn together by Rochelle's soft command,
Thousands of bold custodians gathered,
Dressed in their armour and carrying swords,
A most war-like host filled the *Calypso,*
Stood proud in the sarcophagus chambers,
Awaiting their captain's promised orders.
These chambers were not as decorated
As that belonging to Sigmund alone;

The   sarcophagi   of   the   engineers
Lay   beneath   a   thick   lattice   of   pipework,
Power   cables   and   cold,   empty   bulkheads;
A   few   token   icons   flew   overhead,
Woven   into   martial   flags   depicting
The   bold   symbol   of   the   custodians:
A   sword   set   into   an   empty   circle,
But   otherwise,   all   there   was   practical;
The   *Calypso*'s   veins   and   innards   exposed
Without   any   kind   of   affectation.
There,   beside   Rochelle's   tomb,   stood   the   captain,
Her   armour   as   unadorned   as   the   walls,
And   there,   her   noble   brow   furrowed,   she   spake:
"The   *Calypso*   is   not   a   paradise.
There   is   little   leisure   within   these   walls;
All   here   is   rote   tradition   and   duty.
The   flowers   today   were   made   of   plastic;
The   sky   was   no   more   than   a   projection;
The   sunshine   was   wasteful   golden   streamers;
The   food   was   recycled   nutrition   blocks
Disguised   with   seasoning   to   seem   Earthly;
The   songs   sung   and   stories   told   were   copies
Of   songs   and   stories   never   meant   for   us;
All   the   supposed   culture   we   have   here
Is   a   tired   echo   taught   by   our   teachers.
My   friends,   we   have   an   opportunity,
In   full   respect   of   Sigmund's   great   vision,
To   create   our   own   paradise   as   well.
But   paradise   is   not   found   in   blind   faith,
In   zealously   following   tradition;
If   we   are   to   make   our   own   paradise
Then   we   must   seize   upon   the   means   we   have,
Not   for   our   sakes,   but   for   our   children's   sakes,
So   that   they   are   not   condemned   to   just   watching

The colonists enjoy their paradise.
This, I propose to you custodians:
That our first duty will be as always
To safeguard Sigmund's most hallowed vision,
But that we should also strive for ourselves,
And deliver our children a future
Where they might live in their own paradise.
The means to do this is within our grasp:
It is our job to guard the engineers,
But what we are really watching over
Is their variety of knowledges;
Therefore, I ask you, what would it matter
If we preserved all of those knowledges
Not in these temporal sarcophagi
But in our minds and those of our children,
Blessing our offspring with the expertise
Needed to build a new world of their own;
Not the new world itself, but somewhere else,
Perhaps one of its many splendid moons,
Where they might live in as much luxury
As the colonists on the world below.
What say you, my fellow custodians?
Shall we begin to wake the engineers?
Shall we learn all of their expertises?
Shall we offer our children a future?"
There was no great raucous cheer in response
As there was to George's speech not long past,
Only the rhythmic stamp of boots on steel
As the custodians declared assent,
Choosing to obey their captain's command.
Only one brave soul did not sound assent;
He, a mere young lieutenant, kept his faith,
Waiting for the first opportunity
To slip away from the united crowds.

His moment came when all began action,
Reverently opening the first tomb
Much to the lieutenant's dismayed horror.
The lieutenant rushed away through the ship,
Boots skipping sparks across the metal floors
All the way to George's humble chambers
Where he awoke the slumbering leader
With his descriptions of rebellion;
The custodians had turned on king George,
Rejecting their role as brave overseers
In a misguided and selfish attempt
At improving the lives of their children.
George immediately leapt to action,
Summoning all his loyal advisors
And rousing the *Calypso*'s royal guard;
They came to him quickly at his chambers,
Gathered at the humble hall he called home,
Frightened by rumours of rebellion;
George promptly dismissed their fears, rallied them
And bade them ready themselves for conflict.
The advisors wore simple robes adorned
With the symbols of each of their factions
And at their leader's command, they sharpened,
Offering their cleverness up to him;
The royal guard formed lines at George's command,
Their armour richly inscribed and regal,
Kept finely polished to a mirror shine,
Their sheathed swords, sharp enough to cut diamond,
Now awaiting the order to be drawn.
The rebellion must be quashed swiftly,
That much was clear, but most importantly,
Those once guarded by the custodians
Must be securely guarded against them.
With clarity of purpose, king George marched,

And the decks of the *Calypso* trembled
Beneath the boots of his almighty host;
First, they came to Sigmund's sarcophagus,
Guarded by a pair of custodians;
Merciful George bid them to surrender,
But both refused, despite the king's huge host,
Choosing instead to draw swords and rebel
In the name of their traitorous captain.
The royal guard ascended the dais,
And slew the two rebel custodians
Spilling their blood across the steps inlaid
At both sides of Sigmund's sarcophagus.
Wise George then evacuated the room,
Sealing its every possible entrance
With bulkhead doors thick enough to repel
Anything the custodians might try.
Posting royal guards at each sealed bulkhead,
George did not pause to revel in success,
Marching swiftly on through the *Calypso*,
To the verdant wilderness at her heart,
For the *Calypso* had a forest then,
Made entirely of a creeping vine
Made so virulently and robustly
That it had consumed a great many decks.
Into this thick morass waded king George,
His guard hacking a route through the forest,
Though all still stumbled, made clumsy by it,
To reach the sarcophagus at its core.
For the forest of vines had a secret
Known only to the *Calypso*'s leaders
And those whose duty it was to guard it:
The forest was home to the engineer
Whose most profound purpose would be to wake
And catalyse the new world into life;

Sacred Catherine slept among the vines,
Alone and separate from the others;
So vital that she was strictly guarded
By a detachment of custodians.
Those guardians were now rebels, George knew,
But still he called out to them in mercy,
Offering them a chance to surrender.
When no reply came, he marched deeper still,
To the humid core of the vine forest;
There, the custodians had set some traps
Meant to confound and murder George's guard.
Only, George's advisors were too wise;
They had foreseen the custodians' plans
And each trap was disarmed with utmost care;
The custodians fell upon the guard,
Hacking with dull blades, their armour painted
So that they blended in with the forest;
They fought savagely and caused many wounds,
But were no match for the noble king's guard
Whose flashing pale blades severed vines and veins,
Sundering the custodian rebels.
Having cleared the path, George came to the tomb
Where Catherine slumbered; he was relieved,
For her sarcophagus remained untouched,
Tangled still in her own virulent vines.
He ordered the forest quelled and sealed shut,
With Catherine still at its verdant heart;
Once again closing it behind bulkheads
And posting royal guards at each entrance.
With Sigmund and Catherine now secured
It was time to face the rebellion;
George gathered all his forces together,
Uniting the crew under his banner
And with tremendous force of arms he stormed

The length of the *Calypso*'s splendid arc,
His faith in Sigmund's hallowed vision fierce
In the face of such dreadful betrayal.
With such a clamour of armour and boots
Synchronised to a war-like marching song
Did George and his host arrive finally
At the custodians' thick-walled fortress,
Wherein they were waking the engineers;
One last time, George offered them clemency,
Allowing the rebels to surrender,
And once again no answer was given;
His heart heavy, George ordered the attack
And his brilliant forces surged forward,
Their blades and faces bright with righteousness,
Slaying all rebels who stood before them.
The battle for the gate was swiftly won,
And George swept inside, among empty tombs
Where not long ago, engineers had slept;
The bulk of the rebels had retreated
Taking with them all of the engineers.
George wept then, for he knew that he had failed,
Too late he had arrived to safeguard them,
And he knew all too well the protocol:
That once woken from their sarcophagi,
The engineers could not return to sleep.
The best now he could hope for was rescue:
To hunt down the custodian rebels
And take back from them the poor engineers
Roused from their slumber centuries early.
Yet as George wept, an advisor approached,
Telling him that there was still some good news:
A single engineer remained interred,
Slumbering still while all the others woke;
Roused from his deep grief, George went to her tomb

And saw that it was Rochelle who remained,
Namesake of the custodians' captain
And she whose job it would be to question
Sigmund's splendid vision for the new world.
The gesture was deliberate, he knew:
The rebels had left her here on purpose
Believing that she would be one of them
And fight for their cause upon arrival;
But George was glad, for he knew they were wrong:
Rochelle was not Sigmund's opposition
But an essential part of his vision:
Her questions would help him to refine it,
Correcting any flaws left to be found;
Rochelle would make the new world more perfect
Than it would be by Sigmund's hand alone.
Rejoicing for this minor victory,
George secured the sarcophagus chambers,
Protecting Rochelle with as much fervour
As he had done for both of the others;
Sealing its bulkheads and posting soldiers
To prevent rebellious incursion.
With Rochelle, Sigmund and Catherine safe
He evacuated their entire deck,
Quarantining them, so as to be sure
That no other rebellions would rise
In the long centuries still to occur
Before their arrival at the new world.
This done, George gathered his forces again,
Directing them to track down the rebels
And rescue the awoken engineers.
So began a long and bloody campaign,
Chasing the custodians through the ship;
The chiming of swords meeting resounded,
Ragged bodies fell in droves, cut aside,

And the *Calypso*'s halls were scored and scarred,
Etched deep, as if she herself was wounded;
Yet George did not relent, pushing harder
Through an endless stream of bloody conflict;
No matter how many rebels he slew
There always seemed to be more in hiding,
And no matter how many he captured,
They hid the stolen engineers too well.
George was winning, that much was apparent,
Even when the rebels tried dark tactics,
Resorting to belching, stinking firearms,
Those most dreadful and forbidden weapons
Threatening *Calypso*'s integrity,
George faced them down and deconstructed them
Before any could compromise the hull.
As the war stretched on, George's host suffered,
The crew's usual cycles disrupted
To compensate for the ever-changing
Tides of conflict enveloping the ship.
A decade deep into the weary war
And George gathered his advisors to him;
Not one engineer had been recovered,
And those rebels that remained were cunning,
Battle-hardened and willing to fight on
All the way through the void to the new world;
George told his advisors that he was tired,
That the conflict had drained everybody;
It was time to put aside victory
And consider some kind of compromise;
How, he asked, might we end this endless war.
Together with his advisors, he planned
A means by which the conflict might die down,
And with new resolve warming his old heart
George gave the command to action that plan.

The battles that ensued were directed,
Slowly forcing the rebels to retreat
Across the great arc of the *Calypso*
Towards a singular section of ship;
That section had been emptied of all things
Which might provide any kind of comfort;
The walls and floors and archways were naked,
All windows were welded shut or removed,
The environmental controls were locked
So that it was always too warm or cold,
And the lights were made dim and flickering.
To this dungeon, the rebels were corralled,
Every insurgent forced to live inside
A wretched and unforgiving section
Until they surrendered the engineers.
Victorious in penning the rebels,
The war that had echoed through the tall halls
Now calmed while all awaited the response
From the custodians in their harsh cell;
In the end, it was Rochelle who came forth,
That dire captain who ignited the war
With promises of a new paradise;
Well scarred by conflict herself, she arrived
Alone to come to terms with tired king George.
Her forces were satisfied, she told him,
To live in the dread dungeon provided,
Learning from the awoken engineers
All the knowledges needed to create
A world for themselves and for their children;
She was also satisfied by the way
George had sealed away those three asleep;
She had not come to surrender, she said,
Or to give away any engineers;
Instead, she had come with a proposal:

In return for a supply of rations,
She would be willing to share their knowledge;
In return for a steady stream of food,
The rebels would pass along expertise:
The things they would learn from the engineers.
Worn down to his very bones, George agreed
And Rochelle returned to her dungeon cell,
Through gates now left very slightly ajar,
And so life slowly returned to normal
For the grateful crew of the *Calypso*;
They repaired the damages of the war,
Painting over the worst with bright murals
Of those engineers woken too early,
And even some of those still slumbering;
They counted and named and reclaimed the dead,
Recycling their remains with deep respect,
And melted down their armour and weapons
For reuse in more practical repairs.
Soon, the parks were filled with people again,
Flying kites up among the ship's sky vents,
And king George was grateful to see it all
Returned to how it was before the war
Before he finally died of old age,
His remains reverently recycled
With all the honours the crew could give him;
New kings and queens and officers arose,
Continuing George's great legacy,
Guarding the three remaining engineers
And watching over the gates, still ajar,
That led to rebels' grim dark domain;
Of those rebels, not a great deal is known;
A trickle of knowledges did emerge
In return for a trickle of supplies,
But those knowledges were always piecemeal,

Incomplete and often almost useless,
Claimed, no doubt, from unwilling engineers
Enraged at having been woken early.
Still, we know a few of their victories:
The rebels learned of drone technologies
And used them to make metallic servants
To obey their every whim and bidding;
They learned enough geoengineering
To create crude, first-generation growths
And sustain themselves on the shoddy things;
And they learned how to adapt the nanites
That had been meant to cloud the new world's skies
Into eerie silvery nanite baths
That would constantly repair their bodies,
Giving a chosen few much prolonged lives;
In this way, while generations perished,
Some few lived on, trapped in their silver baths,
Living horrible, indefinite lives.
Of what happened to the rebel captain,
Nothing is known; no doubt she died herself,
Passing the captaincy to those dire lords
Lounging in their quicksilver nanite thrones.
The centuries passed with the war quiet,
Alive now only in song and the scars
Still etched across the *Calypso*'s bulkheads,
Until, at last, her long journey ended
With her arrival above the new world.
It would be easy to describe to you
That hallowed, most celebrated event;
However, that momentous occasion
Is worthy of its own splendid poem,
While this story is almost at its end.
Upon her arrival at the new world,
The *Calypso*'s halls resounded loudly

With the celebrations of all her crew;
All, that is, except for the grim rebels
Who remained silent in their dark dungeon.
Years passed by in joyful preparation,
Orbiting the new world and readying
The *Calypso* for the awakening
Of those three engineers still slumbering.
Only, one day, there was a shuddering
Which trembled through all of the *Calypso,*
And with a great grinding, she broke open;
A huge piece of her had come free, arcing
Slowly towards one of the new world's moons.
In awe, all watched as the rebels landed
Upon that distant moon, having taken
Their entire confined section of the ship.
In awe, all watched in the proceeding years
As lights flickered across that moon's surface;
The rebels were alive, then, and working
To carry out their ill-considered plan.
So ends the tale of the *Calypso*'s war,
As, with the departure of the rebels,
They were swiftly erased from memory,
Existing now only as this story
And the glinting of the lights on their moon.

I have a few tattoos etched into me
Like a kind of physical memory:
Personal works of art to remind me.
Deliberate, vivid, colourful scars.

Inked across my ribs is a crucifix.
It is inscribed to the left, near my heart;
The needling as it was scarred into me
Made me think of Christ's prickling crown of thorns.

The silhouettes of pines across my thigh
Remind me of the rewilded lowlands;
Those barren, overgrazed hills and valleys
Allowed to be reclaimed by Scottish trees.

The feather on my wrist is for Benson,
The cat on my ankle is for Ciara,
And the sunflower on my shoulder blade
Is for their father – my husband, Jakob.

I met Jakob while I was travelling,
Catching my breath between years of study
By crossing Europe on a motorbike.
Eventually, I arrived in Norway.

I rented a room at a small hotel
Run by an unassuming bearded man
Out at a remote fjord famed for fishing.
It was winter; I was the only guest.

A hard cold crept in after I arrived
Making the roads nearly unpassible.
My flimsy coat too thin to weather it,
I remained indoors, learning Norwegian.

The nights were long and quiet and lonely
But the hotel was filled with shelves of books;
So many, they were like insulation
Warming me as much as the burning stove.

The proprietor hardly spoke a word,
But helped me with my pronunciation
As I slowly read through his libraries.
It took me a week to tease out his name.

Jakob did not speak a word of English
So I began to teach him in return
For his help with my fledgling Norwegian.
We progressed slowly, but the nights were long.

One night, he came to me, expressionless
And asked me, in English, to follow him.
He gave me a thick winter coat and boots
And by torchlight led us down to the fjord.

I remember the fierce stars that night,
And the hard white fjord, bright in the moonlight.
There was rime on the trees, frost hanging sharp
And Jakob's breath, freezing into his beard.

At the edge of the fjord we sat, silent.
Jakob switched off his torch and bowed his head,
And it felt like a moment out of time:
As if the whole world had frozen solid.

Suddenly, there was a mighty cracking;
A sound like a protracted thundering
Echoing across the glimmering fjord:
Loud like a whip-crack or sustained gunfire.

The echoes took a while to dissipate,
Only to be followed by another
Catastrophic crackling in succession;
One after the other, the noises came.

I reached out for Jakob: an ice statue
With eyes agleam in the crackling dark,
And when I asked him what the noises were
He told me that they were the voice of God.

Of course it was only the hardened ice,
But right then I was willing to believe;
To sit and listen and maybe discern
Words and meaning in the cacophony.

When I asked Jakob what God was saying,
Jakob only shrugged, his face softening.
He put his arm around me to warm me,
And his beard tickled at my exposed cheek.

I fell in love with him later that week.
We were out in the forest, practising
Our newly forming vocabularies
When we came to a frozen waterfall.

The winter sun was refracting through it.
Jakob pointed at the scattered sunbeams,
Broken into a circle of bright shards,
And declared it to be a sunflower.

His poem done, the herald is silent.
He slouches beside me with his head bowed
As if the story of *Calypso*'s war
Has diminished him with its oration.

The last echoes of his tale cease stirring,
Leaving in their wake a quiet stillness.
Calypso's arches are tall above me
And her hallway stretches out before me.

This is the very same stillness, I think,
As that night out at the fjord with Jakob:
That potent moment before the crackling
That sounded so much like God was speaking.

I raise myself to my feet and advance.
There are windows overlooking the world
And I stand before one, admiring it,
Searching its oceans, its forests, for God.

But God is the new world, I realise:
God is the nanite clouds, and the bright sun,
And the *Calypso* overlooking all.
I am God's voice in this distant system.

The glittering moon, New Terra, arrives,
Emerging darkly from the nanite clouds,
Eclipsing the new world's verdant splendour
With its glinting, shifting, blackened surface.

Its inhabitants, those selfish rebels,
Have proven ultimately impotent;
Their small moon is no more than a shadow
Cast over the resplendent new world's seas.

New Terra vanishes into the clouds
And my sympathy dissipates with it.
The rebels could have ruined the new world,
But for the great faith of the loyalists.

I return to the herald and hold him,
Kissing his hands and cheeks in gratitude.
He gives me a weary smile in return,
Wishing me well though his voice is now hoarse.

It is time for me to confront Sigmund.
Yet first I return to my small chapel,
Where waits my crude cross among plastic plants,
Silhouetted against the sharp white sky.

There, I kneel among the crafted cushions.
There are no candles on the *Calypso*;
A naked flame would be a waste of fuel,
So I light a small candle in my mind.

I did not know the other engineers
But it seems right that I should pray for them.
I hope that they are with us now, watching
Our progress in spite of their absences.

I pray that they found happiness awake,
That they lived long lives on the *Calypso*,
And that they died comfortably, among friends;
Surrounded by those beloved to them.

I find myself thinking about Ciara,
The flowers dripping petals all down her
As she lay there in her hospital bed.
Distracted from my prayer, my words stumble.

There is nobody that will mourn for me,
I realise; my loved ones are all dead:
Jakob, Ciara, Benson and Catherine.
Who is left to light a candle for me?

Watch closely as the young man named Arthur Sigmund
Slowly dons an enormous, rubbery space suit.
It is ribbed and spongy and overinflated
So that when he stands, he nearly topples over.
Beyond the airlock is an expanse of white sky
Lit by a sun slightly brighter than that on Earth;
Upon the endless white clouds bob dirigibles,
An entire city floating on silver balloons,
Tethered together with lengths of metal cable
And occasionally bouncing off each other.
Arthur waddles comically to the airlock door,
And when it whisks open, he steps into the sky.
He is close enough to the surface of Venus
That the gravity is comfortable, nearly Earth.
The balcony beyond the airlock feels unsafe;
It lacks a railing for Arthur to hold on to,
So he teeters at the edge, tether tight in hand.
This city is the first Venusian settlement,
Inhabited exclusively by scientists
Engaging in geoengineering projects,
Preparing Venus for its metamorphosis
From an overheated, thickly toxic wasteland
To another green and blue mirror of Terra.
The atmosphere is still thick enough to float on;
A greenhouse shrouding the distant surface below,
Where mining drones toil at the rich, rocky surface,
Exploiting it for its useful materials.
Arthur has come to witness a major event,

The first stage in geoengineering Venus;
There is little time left until it commences,
So he takes a waddling leap from the balcony,
Falling ungracefully into the atmosphere.
The thick clouds envelop him immediately,
But he slows to a bobbing halt quickly enough,
The ultralight gasses in his suit buoying him
So that he is a miniature dirigible,
Floating easy and free on the thick white cloudscape.
For a while he simply lays there, prone on his back,
Before clumsily paddling with his arms and legs
Until he is facing the sun. His visor dims.
The timer at the corner of his visor stops
And a great shape in the sky comes into focus.
An enormous octagon eclipses the sun,
Wheeling like an escaped umbrella on the wind.
When it has encompassed the sun entirely,
The octagon shifts – plated mirrors focusing
Until the sun once again shines over Venus.
The sun is slightly less bright than it was before;
That magnificent, gargantuan space mirror
Has begun the process of cooling Venus down:
Reducing the greenhouse effect on the planet
In an effort to slowly thin the atmosphere.
In a few years, the floating city will be gone
And there will be a base on the planet's surface;
There are plans to bring nitrogen from Jupiter,
And to tow whole seas of water from Europa,
Until, one day, possibly in Arthur's lifetime,
Venus is rendered completely habitable.
With much wobbling and struggling, Arthur rolls himself
So that he is facing downwards, towards Venus.
There is nothing but the thick atmosphere to see,
So he closes his eyes and imagines instead:

Those shining, reflective blues and whites, and rich greens.
Yet, instead of elation, Arthur feels sorrow.
Venus is going to be yet another Earth,
Just like Mars is – all the worst of humanity
Slowly being spread across the solar system.
The problem, he thinks, are the ideologies
Embedded so deep in human disposition:
Capitalism and useless superstition;
Racism and sexism ingrained so deeply.
Venus will undoubtedly be a work of art,
But its inhabitants will bring ugly ideas,
Inherited from their parents and ancestors.
It would be better to start again, Arthur thinks:
To engineer a new world for a new people
Free of the great burden of human history.
Arthur remains where he is for a while longer,
Wondering at his own curious idea.
It would be a truly epic experiment
To engineer a new world and colonise it
With blank humans, unaware of their heritage.
Eventually, he begins to haul himself up,
Back towards the floating dirigible city,
Yet as he goes he finds that his thoughts are whirring.
Arthur has never been inspired like this before.

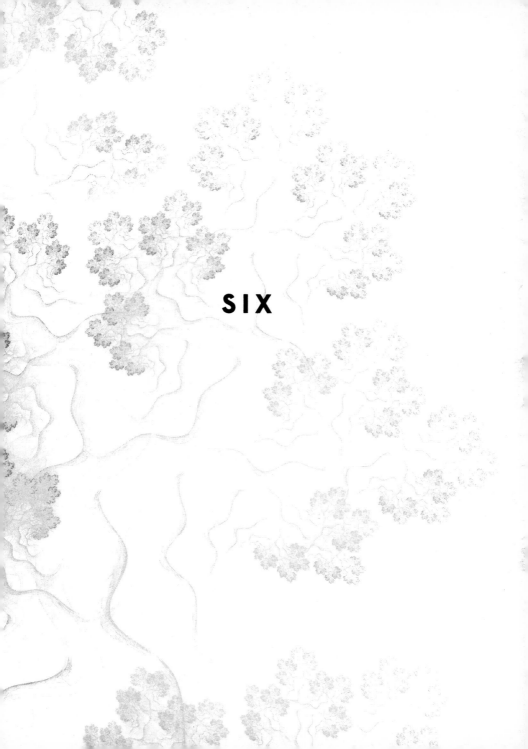

SIX

The tall halls of the *Calypso* resound
With the joyous voices of all her crew
As they decorate her silver arches
With blooms of plastic flowers and bright paints.

Where I walk they pave the way with petals,
Decorating me with garlands and crowns
Wreathed of plastic grasses and marbled beads
Until I am as vivid as the walls.

Beyond the windows the new world revolves
So richly green that it looks overgrown,
So shining blue its oceans might be glass,
So crisply white its clouds might be cotton.

Freshly painted portraits adorn bulkheads,
Each depicting Catherine's sacrifice;
Her transcendence from human to garden
Artfully rendered by the faithful crew.

The portraits of Catherine bother me
Because they make her look benevolent;
None of them have managed to capture her
The way she was: the forthright scientist.

I stop among the celebrating crowds,
Pausing in my journey to find Sigmund,
Suddenly weary with the way I am,
My heart a heavy red stone in my chest.

I want to be as joyful as the crew;
I want to feel their noisy elation,
To have my blood run quickly through my veins,
To soften my heart and feel it beating.

I remember Catherine's gift to me,
Those rainbow capsules still in my pocket.
Rolling a sparkling pill onto my palm,
I swallow it without hesitation.

    Something lifts in me immediately
As a warmth spreads through me from my stomach;
It is a bit like drinking strong liquor.
Strolling on through the crowds, I feel lighter.

    The warmth reaches the ends of my fingers,
Tingling my toes as I walk through petals.
Suddenly, I want to remove my shoes,
So I do – advancing barefoot instead.

    Everything around me seems brighter now;
I catch the tune of a song and sing it
Wordlessly signalling my elation
As the warmth increases in intensity
Like I am drunk but not drunk more like sober
Like I have been asleep for days and woken wide
    I stride each swing of my step cascading petals
        thinking of warm nights in Norway with Jacob
            the way we would drink fine whisky some nights
                our warm delirium indistinguishable from love
                but this is not delirium this is
                something like awesome clarity
                not a thinking but a knowing
                suddenly I see Catherine's smile
                all her eyes upon me
                watching from the walls
                this martyr, my friend
                but she was human
                I tell the crew I stop them
                tell them she was a person
                not this deified
                Christ-like arms-wide

they take my hands dance me

spin me through the petals drape me

their joy becoming my joy and maybe this

this is how it felt to know Christ in person

just a man just a man named Jesus

just a man who walked barefoot sometimes smiled sometimes

I wonder if He told jokes

sneezed yawned had bad days

skin scarred by His work His work

just a carpenter just a man

just a saviour just the son of God

who died for all of us

told jokes sometimes

Catherine she was just a girl

just a woman who danced

planted plants

wept when she said goodbye

just a botanist just a girl

just a catalyst who died for the colonists

gave them a garden her gift the garden

just a martyr who

danced

I dance for her now

laugh and love her

lucky enough to know her

the girl with kaleidoscope eyes

who laughed sometimes

I volunteered at a homeless shelter
When I was sixteen, washing weary feet,
Dishing out hot broth and cups of coffee,
Changing the bedding on the bunks each day.

I saw the true face of addiction, there;
The relief drugs offer to the helpless,
First enslaving them emotionally,
Then chemically as their bodies adapt.

There were AA meetings and I would go,
Watching the same faces keep relapsing,
Picking up their one day, one week tokens
Like they were building up a collection.

A friend of mine went on a trip to Mars,
Volunteering with a charity there,
And she returned with similar stories:
The marginalised living in shelters.

I suppose I thought that Mars was perfect:
A distant, flawless, fresh utopia,
As if Mars was Heaven and Earth was Hell.
My friend's stories were a revelation.

There were homeless people living on Mars;
Some mentally unwell, others addicts,
Displaced by an indifferent culture
Capable but unwilling to help them;

As if autonomy is a virtue;
As if a man should help himself alone;
As if a woman is only worthy
Of her health if she earned it by herself.

I began to research Mars and its flaws,
Addicted to reading bleak articles
Detailing humanity's failures
Repeating themselves on another world.

The worst article was about seagulls.
It took decades to design them for Mars,
Adapting them for weaker gravity
And a marginally colder climate.

The gulls thrived, but not due to their design.
They thrived because they themselves adapted,
Leaving coastal towns for inland landfills
And there pecking at humanity's filth.

The pictures haunted me for weeks after;
Landfills filling ancient Martian craters,
Speckled with tiny dark winged silhouettes;
The birds' corruption preceding their birth.

The comedown from Catherine's pill is worse
Than it was from her rainbow infusion,
Making me feel so sluggish and clumsy
That I have to concentrate on walking.

It would be easy to take another;
To regain that enhanced cognition high,
But I only have two rainbow pills left
And I can feel myself court addiction.

Best save them for when I need them the most;
When I need an absolute clarity,
Not just a means of escaping a slump.
Swallowing that last capsule was foolish.

The crew support me the rest of the way,
Arms around my waist almost carry me
So that I feel as if I am floating
Above a plastic petal-strewn meadow.

And even though my skin feels too heavy,
My heart struggling to push my blood through me,
The crew's joy remains infectious enough
That I can feel my smile stick to my face.

At last, I arrive at the colonists,
Their chambers refrigerated enough
That the cold metal floor bites sharp at me.
The crew slide sandals onto my bare feet.

There are thousands here, waiting to be born;
Curled up foetally and hanging from racks
Are silhouetted human shapes in sacs,
As if *Calypso* has thousands of wombs.

The sacs are all the colour of amber
Making the colonists look like insects
Trapped in tree sap thousands of years ago,
Which is not far from the truth, I suppose.

There are smaller and larger silhouettes,
Men and women of all shapes and sizes,
But no children are visible – not yet;
It will be for them to provide their own.

They will be born simultaneously,
Which makes me think about astrology,
That ancient alchemy I dabbled in
Back in my early teens – a silly phase.

To think, though: thousands with the same birth chart,
All of their horoscopes identical,
Their destinies in perfect alignment.
It would fascinate the ancient mystics.

But, of course, we are far away from Earth.
The new world will have new constellations,
Multiple moons swing about its heavens,
And different planets dance in its sky.

My smile widens as I imagine them,
The colonists looking up at the night,
Seeing patterns in all those tiny lights
And naming them – giving the stars meaning.

This. These people. This is why I am here,
Why I left everything I knew behind:
To wake these new people, and to help them;
To give them the gift of Earthly knowledge.

I stumble forward, still feeling weakened,
But none of the crew advance through with me.
They wait at the entrance, wide eyes watching,
Expecting me to go on by myself.

I shiver, huddled up among the racks,
Following a distant sound: hammering,
Resounding through the quiet, humming halls.
Soon, I am alone with the colonists.

A figure comes into view. Hammer raised,
Sigmund pauses as he notices me,
Then gently places the hammer aside.
The last echoes of his striking recede.

We stand there a while, he and I, silent,
And his expression is unreadable.
Then, he raises his arms and advances,
Folding me in a ritual embrace.

His voice is soft in my ear as he speaks.
"Are you ready?" he asks. His breath is hot.
I tell him that I am indeed ready,
But I feel my smile fading from my face.

The last time I landed on the new world
It was a barren and blasted wasteland.
This time, it is a lush, living garden,
Wreathed in white clouds and bursting with wildlife.

There is a series of metallic scrapes;
The clamps holding this section of the ship
Disengage. Thrusters ignite around us,
Pushing us from *Calypso*'s circumference.

      A mere shuttle would not be big enough
To transport the thousands of colonists,
So we are launching a piece of the ship
And descending to the surface in it.

      Only we two, Sigmund and me, are here.
This journey is for us alone to take:
The last of the *Calypso*'s engineers
Tasked with delivering the colonists.

      I do feel somewhat sorry for the crew;
That they will never land on the new world,
Forever confined to the *Calypso*,
Breathing recycled air their entire lives.

      But the new world was never meant for them.
It is a planet for a new people
Uncorrupted by humanity's past:
A people capable of new ideas.

      The colonists have been designed as such;
They are a blank people, memoryless,
But blessed with the capacity to learn
At a greatly accelerated rate.

      They will develop their first language fast,
And with their words they will describe their world,
Codifying its every element
And solidifying it for themselves.

      We will leave them no clothes or devices;
Or tools, or instructions, or directions;
The colonists will develop their own
Without any help from their creators.

Sigmund, strapped into his seat beside me,
Monitors our descent through the heavens,
And for a while I watch him as he works,
Considering our great disagreement.

Sigmund believes in utter ignorance;
That the colonists should be unaware
Of their lineage – that they come from Earth.
That such knowledge would be a detriment.

I, however, believe differently;
That the colonists should know about us
And be told about human history
So that they can learn from all our mistakes.

Sigmund believes that I would corrupt them,
That the simple knowledge of history
Would be enough for them to repeat it,
Dooming them from the moment of their birth.

It is for me to argue otherwise,
To perhaps even find a compromise,
Teaching the colonists some small lessons
Learned by humans over millennia.

To Sigmund the colonists are seagulls,
And human history is the landfill
That would ruin them were they to find it,
But I have more faith in them than he does.

It must be said that I do admire him.
My presence here speaks to how wise he is:
He could have led his mission unopposed,
But he invited a voice of dissent.

A true expert knows the worth of debate
To test the strength of a hypothesis:
That if he can successfully argue
Against me, it reinforces his claims.

I represent the unknown to Sigmund,
The very limits of his expertise,
Because I have something that he does not:
I have faith in an ever-loving God.

The clouds engulfing our huge transport part
And there before us is the bright new world,
Not yet named because we will not name it.
That honoured task is for the colonists.

As we leave the *Calypso*'s gravity,
Trading it for the new world's heavy pull,
I pray for all those waiting behind me;
The thousands that we are delivering.

I am jarred in my seat as we descend,
Hitting the new world's thickened atmosphere,
Giving us a bright tail like a comet,
The viewscreens flashing white as we push through.

Then we are among clouds – the new world's clouds,
Made of water vapour and not nanites,
So that they swirl soundlessly across us,
Obscuring our view of the land below.

My exoskeleton whirs as we fall
Compensating for all the gravities
Making me heavier and heavier;
I can feel it pressed up against my skin.

There is a jolt – the landing thrusters fire,
Suddenly slowing our hurtling descent,
So that we leave the new world's clouds gently,
Revealing the surface, so close below.

For a moment, I find myself baffled,
Wondering how we have returned to Earth;
Somewhere in Northern Europe, I think – France,
With all its verdant greenery; soft shores.

There is an enormous river delta
Composed of emerald green shard islands
And to either side of it are lowlands
Composed of clumped forests and long meadows.

The sea, or maybe an ocean, sparkles,
But there is a strangeness about the view:
That long coastline ends far too abruptly;
The land does not have any beaches yet.

In time, I know that there will be beaches.
Erosion will happen, just like on Earth,
Tides tumbling rocks and wearing down pebbles
To form grains that will feel soft beneath feet.

The new world's pull is unEarthly as well,
Its gravity like a hand gripping me,
Trying to force me to fall from the sky
And pull me inwards and into itself.

I would never be comfortable down here,
Always struggling under my own weight,
Pressed hard against my exoskeleton,
My lungs working twice as hard just to breathe.

But for the colonists, this will be home.
They are designed to be adaptable,
Skeletons and organs developing
So that they will thrive in this gravity.

The transport tips so that we will land flat
And my view is suddenly of the sky,
A shade of blue not quite the same as Earth;
Lighter, maybe, with touches of orange.

I concentrate on making myself breathe
Despite the new weight gripping at my lungs.
It feels like all my blood is in my feet;
Like my heart is struggling to draw it up.

With another jolt the transport settles,
Giving me a view of rolling green hills
Adorned with verdant copses and forests
And speckled with the silhouettes of birds.

This, then, is the new world now completed,
Composed of Catherine's cataclysm
And Sigmund's heavenly machinations;
The *Calypso*'s bounty manifested.

These fields, these forests await occupants.
Even from here I can see the great fruits,
Ripened and engorged, hanging from the trees,
Ready for newborn hands to reach and pluck.

I stand and help Sigmund from his own seat,
Feeling the tremble running through his hands.
He stretches, eyes agleam in the sunlight;
For a moment I see the boy he was.

"The new atmosphere is unsafe for us,"
He tells me, as he pulls his helmet on,
"But the colonists will adapt quickly.
It will only take them a few lungfuls."

I enclose myself in my own helmet,
Sigmund's voice crackling in my ear instead.
"The process is mostly automated,"
He says. "We only need to supervise."

The lander begins to depressurise,
Trading our Earthly air for the new world's
Until a red light flashes in my helm,
Warning me of the air's toxicity.

We wait before the lander's rear bulkheads
While they gradually part, grinding open
And revealing the open hills beyond.
A cool breeze rushes inside, chilling me.

And despite the grand nature of our task,
We leave the colonists for a small while
And step out onto the rich green grasses,
Disturbing beetles and mice with our boots.

This is an indulgence, to be out here.
I find a flower and touch its petals,
Stare a while up at that enormous sky,
Mount a hill and admire the distant sea.

The horizon seems too far away, here;
The new world's prodigious circumference
Providing me with a much longer view
Than any I ever had back on Earth.

I want so badly to remove my helm;
To feel the air across my exposed skin;
To lay in the grasses and pluck the blades,
Knotting them into a grassy green crown.

I see Sigmund examining a rock
Which protrudes sharply, covered in mosses.
"Beautiful," he says. "Simply beautiful.
It's even better than I imagined."

He crouches down and rolls a rock over,
Then raises a palm full of writhing worms.
For a while he is silent, watching them,
Before returning them to the rich soil.

"Come, then," he says, and his voice sounds softer,
As if he has witnessed a miracle
And the sight of it still burns within him.
"Time to wake the new world's inhabitants."

Initiation proves to be simple,
Although it does require two engineers,
We each pressing our fingers to touchscreens
And verifying our identities.

As the colonisation commences
I wonder what the procedure would be
Had none of us engineers awoken.
Would the whole mission have been compromised?

    The hull of the transport starts to unfold,
Elegant mechanisms reaching out
As the racks tremble, rolling sacs on rails,
Readying the colonists for their births.

    The sacs are gently handled – sliced and peeled,
Revealing the naked, hairless newborns,
Skins still slick with sacred preservatives,
Not quite dead, but not yet alive either.

    Cushioned machine hands manoeuvre them each,
Decanting them from their discarded wombs;
With warm water they are wiped of the oils,
Leaving their soft and uncalloused skins clear.

    Beside the parted bulkheads they arrive
Flesh punctured by mechanical medics
Pushing rainbow cocktails into their veins;
A different shade to Catherine's mixture.

    A set of panels is pressed to their chests,
Administering a jolt of power;
Delivering the spark that starts their hearts.
The colonists take their first gasping breaths.

    Sigmund watches from the transport's rear ramp,
One foot in the grasses of the new world,
His expression so soft inside his helm.
It is an expression I recognise.

    I remember giving birth to Benson;
The way my husband held my hand so hard,
Otherwise silent as he sat with me;
Jakob was never one to give speeches.

But when he heard Benson's small voice wailing,
It instilled something in him – his eyes changed,
Brows rising in wonder as he beheld
His child, his son, alive and in the world.

Sigmund, too, is silent as he watches,
But he suddenly seems so much older;
A happy but elderly man, humbled
At the sight of his vision realised.

The colonists are placed in the grasses,
Each curled up and still unconscious for now,
Their bodies beginning to awaken
After their long voyage across the stars.

When they open their eyes, we will be gone.
There will be no enormous transport ship,
Only the rolling hills, and the vast sky.
They will never realise we were here.

Unless, that is, we tell them about us:
Teach them that they are a kind of human
Descended from a troubled ancient race,
And show them all the best and worst of us.

But there will be time to do that later.
Better that they wake up for the first time
Alone with each other beneath the stars,
Untroubled by those that engineered them.

One by one, the colonists are laid out
Naked and curled up among the grasses;
First hundreds, and then thousands decanted,
Filling the hills with slumbering figures.

The gentle process goes on for hours,
Until the sun begins to sink at last,
Its brilliant rays casting long shadows
As it dips beyond the most distant hills.

The sky is streaked yellow and then orange
Before blushing a deep, bloody crimson,
Turning the idle clouds afire with light,
Set against a dark, navy blue backdrop.

The first stars emerge, sharp against the dusk,
And the land is lit by the new world's moons.
Four crescents swing through the darkened heavens;
Silver hooks that might catch against the trees.

Sigmund walks among the colonists now,
The twin torches embedded in his helm
Making ribs and fingers and ankles glow
As he studies the slumbering newborns.

There is a weary sigh from the transport
As it finishes its decantation;
Its walls fold back together, task complete,
Leaving us with only the wind's murmur.

Yet as I listen, I hear other sounds:
The soft rushing of the river nearby,
And the calls of nocturnal animals,
And the breathing of all the colonists.

It is time for me and Sigmund to leave,
Yet we both seem hesitant to do so.
I walk among the colonists myself,
Admiring their unlined, newborn features.

There is not a single scar among them,
No frown-lines, or pock-marks, or missing limbs;
A strange thing to see on adult figures.
They are almost as new as the new world.

Finally, as the dark of night takes hold,
We two engineers return to our ship.
Standing on the threshold a moment more,
We join hands, keen to feel each other's grip.

A warning light flashes in my helmet,
Telling me that it is time to depart.
Waiting any more courts catastrophe:
The chance that the colonists might see us.

Returning to the cockpit, we strap in,
Initiating the transport's boosters.
The thrust is sudden and incredible,
Leaving me stunned and breathless as we soar.

With tremendous force we fly for the sky,
Quick enough that I find myself afraid
We might shatter the delicate heavens,
Scattering the stars as we smash through them.

I close my eyes, think of the colonists
And hope that some might awaken in time
To see us rise not as a rocket ship
But as an omen – a bright shooting star.

Back when I was an eco-activist,
Those brief years at the start of my studies,
I made a lot of foolish decisions,
Carried away by my own righteousness.

There is a certain nuance to ethics.
Ideologies are all well and good,
But genuine ethical decisions
Take patience, research and expert debate.

There was an aviary near my school,
Filled with all kinds of endangered species:
Birds of paradise living in cages
For all to come ogle and photograph.

Walking past the place would leave me in tears.
All those beautiful birds beneath a roof,
Unable to spread their wings and soar free,
Trapped in cages, their calls intermingling.

To me, it felt like an avian right
That all birds should have access to the sky.
So, I began a campaign of protest,
Sending letters arguing my beliefs.

The responses, when I got them, were brief.
The birds were endangered, and protected,
And would likely die beyond their cages,
Not equipped for our mild ecosystem.

Of course, this was not good enough for me,
So I started organising protests
Outside the aviary with my friends,
Waving colourful but naïve placards.

'Free the birds!' was our ill-informed slogan,
Catchy enough that more young fools joined us,
Fighting, we thought, on behalf of the birds,
But secretly revelling in themselves.

Eventually our college got involved,
Delivering expert testimonies
On behalf of the poor aviary,
Trying to convince us of our folly.

This was enough to disperse the smartest,
Leaving only myself and two others,
By now fanatical in our beliefs;
Unswayed by anything resembling facts.

In the end, with nobody on our side,
We decided to break in to the place
And open the cages, freeing the birds.
We imagined ourselves heroes to them.

In the dead of night we broke down the door,
Rushing around as the alarm sounded.
We had brought heavy bolt-cutters with us,
But there were no locks barring the cages.

When we opened the cages and windows
Some of the birds flapped free, but most stayed,
Their beady eyes reflecting our torches,
Frightened, perhaps, by all the light and noise.

By the time the authorities arrived
We were gone, laughing, giddy with triumph,
The night filled with flapping, colourful wings
And the calls of exotic bird species.

For a few days afterwards we saw them,
Parrots and cardinals perched on street-lamps,
But the sightings very quickly reduced
As scientists with nets rounded them up.

Quite a few died, as the experts promised,
Their brightly coloured bodies mauled by cats.
And somehow me and my friends were not caught;
Our faked alibis bore their scrutiny.

It took me years to accept I was wrong;
That my beliefs, as noble as they were,
Were misguided – that conviction alone
Does not turn an opinion into fact.

Truly ethical decisions take time.
They take research, and expert opinion,
And peer review, and well-reasoned debate.
One must be willing to be proven wrong.

The hall of lenses is alive with lights.
An array of telescopes is focused,
Magnifying the new world's nuances
And projecting them across those who watch.

The projections are mostly circular,
A tumble of kaleidoscopic lights,
And they remind me of Catherine's eyes,
As if she is looking up at us all.

The crew shuffle through the hall of lenses.
In a hushed awe they watch the projections:
Close-up slices of the new world's surface
Blurring whenever the telescopes shift.

Our orbit means constant realignment.
While one telescope forms a clear picture
Others swing slowly, searching for focus,
Offering almost random images.

I catch snatches of birds perched in branches,
The heights of tall waves, rising and rolling,
The glowing orange ooze of molten rock,
The shimmer of insect carapaces.

Every now and then a lens finds the light
Cast by the sun across the mirrored sea,
Throwing searing white arcs across the walls
Like silent, crescent flashes of lightning.

Everybody here is waiting to see:
To get the first glimpse of the colonists
As they go about the day of their birth,
Discovering themselves and the new world.

I wonder what they thought of the sunrise;
The flood of sunshine rolling down the hills.
Did they watch in wonder at their first dawn?
Transfixed, perhaps, by that blazing beacon?

Or maybe they danced to herald the sun,
Clean skin glowing; maybe they learned to smile
While they moved together, warming themselves,
Greeting that great celestial vision.

I wonder, too, what they will think of us:
The *Calypso*'s circular silhouette
Passing through the sky like a hollow moon.
Will they etch our image into the soil?

A telescope suddenly focuses,
Projecting the picture of a woman
Watching the water of a river curl
Across the backs of her outstretched fingers.

The hall of lenses stills to a silence
As more images come into focus.
A muddle of precious moments unfolds;
Muscles and chests and faces in motion.

Child-like, the colonists explore themselves.
I catch an image of a man eating,
Juices running down his chin from the fruit,
His eyes wide as he savours its flavours.

A girl rolls in the long grasses, stretching,
Hands curling and uncurling around blades;
She accidentally cuts a finger,
Watching in fascination as she bleeds.

They move so easily and comfortably,
Immediately at home in their world,
Its gravity is now their gravity,
Its atmosphere enriching their bloodstreams.

Yet, not every projection displays peace.
A woman murders a mouse with a rock;
She raises its body triumphantly
And others gather round, fascinated.

Two men fight over a morsel of fruit,
Their shining new bodies scuffed and bruised black.
They roll together in the long grasses,
Trading clumsy blows, the fruit forgotten.

They are human, then, despite the new world;
Undeveloped, and still prone to squabbles.
As the fight unfolds, it draws a small crowd
And I feel a heaviness in my chest.

The colonists need a teacher, I think;
A parental figure to temper them;
Someone to say that violence is wrong,
And explain why it should be avoided.

The hall of lenses quietens further
Until there is only *Calypso*'s hum
And the small glass-ring chimes of the lenses,
Heralding the arrival of Sigmund.

Dressed in a t-shirt and jogging bottoms,
Sigmund seems tired and ready to relax.
He smiles and waves wearily at the crew
Before moving across to stand with me.

The fight is projected across his face;
A tangle of limbs writhing his features
Until the lens loses focus at last,
Blurring green and brown across him instead.

"There's a certain purity about them,"
He says, "don't you think? An untouched beauty.
Still earthly, but without the corruption
That makes the rest of us so horrible."

He could be describing a glacier,
Or a remote, unmaintained wilderness.
I feel inclined to share the obvious
And tell him that "They're fighting each other."

"Of course they are," he says. "They're still human.
But it's a fight for the thrill of the fight.
There's no malice in it – they are alive
And finding new ways to express themselves."

"Through violence, though? They could be better.
We could tell them why violence is wrong;
Teach them even a few simple morals
To help guide them in the right direction."

The light of the lenses casts Sigmund's face
In an ever-shifting whirl of colours.
When he smiles at me, it is distorted,
Sometimes kindly and sometimes sinister.

"I know what you want," Sigmund says to me.
"You want a burning bush to speak to them
And give them ten commandments to follow.
You would lead them from above, like a god."

"No!" I feel my voice rise. I am goaded,
I know, but still I continue: "That's not…"
I take a breath. "I just want to teach them
All the lessons history has taught us."

"They will have their own history," he says.
"They will learn by making their own mistakes.
And they may even invent their own gods.
But we will not be gods to them, Rochelle."

"We don't have to be gods to them," I say.
"We can teach them as parents teach children:
Through the wisdom of our experience,
Not the power of our authority."

"We have no authority any more,"
Sigmund says. "The new world belongs to them."
There is a resolution in his voice
That tells me I am making no progress.

I fall quiet, but I am not perturbed.
This brief exchange, in the hall of lenses,
Bodes well for continued future debate:
We are talking, and that is what matters.

For now, I leave him with his victory,
In the hope that he might reflect, later,
And consider some of my arguments.
I am in no rush, here – debate takes time.

Sigmund puts his arm around my shoulder
And together we watch the colonists
As they learn how to run and laugh and cry.
Every breath they take is a miracle.

On the way back to my little temple
I pass through a vaulted open chamber
Illuminated by the dazzling sun
Which sits like an iris in a porthole.

I notice a moon is transitioning
Providing that great celestial eye
With a pupil – crossing its circumference.
I bask in the warming glow, feeling watched.

Feeling famished, I pause at a café
Where the crew eat iridescent beetles,
Shucking them free of their carapaces
As if they are eating pistachios.

A young man shows me how to break the shells,
Splintering each shimmering carapace
To expose the edible white innards.
With bits of beetle in my teeth, I eat.

Feeling sated, I lean back and digest,
Wondering at the basket of shell bits.
I once read that insects are resistant
To most forms of cosmic radiation.

I imagine recovering the shells,
Sewing them together into a suit
Or maybe a kind of carapace cloak
Composed of all those iridescent shades.

I could explore the new world's moons, perhaps;
Sweeping the regolith with my new cloak,
Protected from the worst of the sun's heat
And the radiation from distant stars.

Eventually I stand and continue,
Wandering through the *Calypso* idly
And considering the years still to come;
The rest of my life, spent on this station.

Or is the *Calypso* more like a moon?
A permanent orbiting satellite
With a discrete set of ecosystems.
She is no longer a starship, at least.

One day soon, I will have to find a place
To make my home – my very own alcove.
I always wanted to live on a beach,
In a cosy cottage with a small dog.

Here, I will have a metal apartment,
Decorated in the style of the crew,
With paints, and projections, and memories
Enriching the cold and naked bulkheads.

I can look down on the new world, at least,
And from time to time take some holidays,
Shuttling across to unexplored moons,
Wearing my shimmering carapace cloak.

Maybe I could contact the New Terrans,
Once my work with Sigmund is concluded,
And attempt to open a dialogue;
Negotiate peace between us and them.

Warmed by the sun, and my meal, and my thoughts,
I finally arrive at my small church,
And there fold myself into the pillows,
Feeling exhausted down to my marrow.

Letting myself relax, I watch the sky
As it writhes around the new world below,
Letting those clouds turn my thoughts vaporous,
As if I might become as light as air.

It feels like a long time since I last slept.
The new world and all its moons spin around,
Curving lazily across my porthole.
Like a child's mobile, they lull me to sleep.

Come, sit with the man who is named Arthur Sigmund
Who is admiring the view from the broad windows
Set into the shuttle's observation chamber.
Before him is mighty Saturn, rings resplendent.
This is the end of a long, seven-month journey
Decelerating most of the way from Luna
After using the gravity slingshot housed there
To deliver transports out to distant planets.
From here, he can see Saturn's strange hexagon storm;
A blue patch with six linear sides at its base.
It looks as if the storm has been designed somehow,
Yet Arthur knows that it is just an illusion;
Saturn's hexagon is at the heart of six storms,
Kept equidistant by the giant's gravity.
Arthur has come here to see Titan's shipping yards,
The place where the *Calypso*'s construction will start.
Titan is still distant from here, yet visible,
Prickled with millions of tiny star-like flares
Cast by the mining drones' magnesium cutters
As they use them to strip the huge moon's resources.
Arthur is restless, sat at the edge of his seat,
It will be hours until he sees the scaffolding
He knows is down there, newly orbiting Titan.
There are already a few heavy transport ships
Casting glows across Saturn's rings with their engines,
Ready to tow the scaffolding back to Terra,
But there are still a few more months left before then,
As the *Calypso*'s superstructure is fleshed out.

Studying the ship's logs, Arthur realises
It will be hours yet until he sees the scaffolding,
So he forces himself to sit back and relax.
Watching Saturn's rings is somewhat meditative
So he focuses on them, admiring their arcs.
Curious, he calls up information on them,
Scrolling through recent geological surveys.
The rings have mostly been found to be ice, he learns,
But not wholly – there are some interesting finds;
Bits of debris embedded in the icy clumps.
From what Arthur reads, it looks like the rings were formed
During a great catastrophe ages ago
After one of Saturn's moons disintegrated
Due to a collision with a huge asteroid,
Or, possibly, another one of Saturn's moons.
Arthur is fascinated by this theory,
Enough that he forgets about the scaffolding;
For a time, he simply watches the rings in awe,
Imagination kindled by the magnitude
Of the stellar catastrophe by which they formed.
Such destruction, and such beauty to follow it.

SEVEN

I dream, and in my dream I am dying.
I am lying in a hospital bed
And through the window I can see the sun
Suspended in the blue – the sun of Earth.

    I am hooked up to some beeping machines
Half obscured by the bunches of flowers
Perched on every available surface,
Dripping their silken petals over me.

    Sounds of human life drift in from outside:
Children at play, dogs barking and sirens,
The crackle of an ill-tuned radio,
Constant footsteps and murmurs and laughter.

    On all sides of me are my family.
There is Ciara, and she is all grown up;
She has brought her husband along with her,
And her children sit and play at my feet.

    Jakob is here as well, looking ancient.
Wrinkled and hunched, he holds on to my hand
Like he might be able to follow me
If he just holds on to me tight enough.

    With every laboured breath, I catch nice scents:
Jakob's overpowering aftershave;
Freshly baked bread, like my mother would make;
All the intermingled flowers' perfumes.

    I know that I do not have much longer,
That my body is about to fail me,
But I am not afraid. I am content;
I have lived a long and fulfilling life.

I think about the job that I turned down
All those years ago, on the *Calypso*,
And I am glad that I never left Earth,
Suspended while all of my loved ones died.

I squeeze Jakob's hand and call for Ciara.
They come closer, and tell me they love me,
Kissing my forehead and hands so softly,
Delivering me gently to my death.

When they part, I see that Benson is here.
He is tall and grey and stern, dressed in white.
I see him smile an affectionless smile
As he drags a drug into a needle.

Too late, I realise why he is here.
Jakob and Ciara pin my frail body,
Pressing me down so that I cannot move.
Benson rolls up my sleeve; his hands are cold.

I am woken by the needle's puncture,
Drenched in sweat, I unclench my fists and breathe,
Untangling myself from my pillow nest
And rising unsteadily to my feet.

Only I keep stumbling, until I fall;
Landing hard against the floor, I am bruised.
The floor has started trembling, I notice,
And the shadows across it are moving.

The *Calypso* sounds different – awake,
Her hum now aggressive, not ambient,
And the nanite clouds engulfing my view
Wisp quickly across the porthole window.

A familiar force pushes me back,
Still gentle, but gradually worsening,
Making it difficult to stand upright.
Inertia – the *Calypso* is moving.

I remember something the herald said:
That she had one more journey left to make,
But I did not think it would be so soon,
Nor do I know our new destination.

Sigmund might be adjusting our orbit,
Finding us a comfortable place to stay
While we watch the new world as it unfolds.
I decide to see if I can find him.

Fighting the inertia, I gain my feet,
Using bulkheads to push myself along
Until I am out in the tall hallway
Where the crew have set up a few railings.

By the time I make my way down the hall
I am exhausted, so I head across
To an open airlock antechamber
And pull on one of the EVA suits.

The exoskeleton whirs, helping me.
I stumble a little more easily,
One boot at a time through the *Calypso*,
Wondering at the heightened inertia.

The *Calypso* is building too much speed
For a simple orbital adjustment.
It feels like all her engines have been lit,
Forcing us so fast through the new world's sky.

The crew seem just as concerned as I am.
Those I see cling hold of the thin railings,
Waiting for the inertia to finish,
But we seem to keep accelerating.

I help who I can, pulling them along
Until we find cushioned seats and alcoves:
Comfortable, safe places to ride it out.
They wind plastic flowers around my suit.

Soon, I am a walking plastic garden,
Hauling myself over to a railway
And commandeering an empty carriage;
It grinds through the *Calypso*'s curved tunnels.

My suit is reading two Earth gravities.
Much more, and the train will come to a halt;
Worse, I will not be able to stand up
Even with the exoskeleton's help.

Luckily, it does not seem to get worse;
We are accelerating steadily
Even as I reach my destination,
A few metres from the *Calypso*'s bridge.

The long tunnel that leads up to the bridge
Is meant to be a kind of transition
From the mild centrifugal gravity
Of the *Calypso*'s arc, to zero G.

I haul myself up the endless ladder
One arm after the other, suit whirring,
Forced hard against the solid metal rungs
Until, at last, I emerge on the bridge.

Where before there were choirs of crewmen
Joyfully controlling the *Calypso*,
Now there is only a skeleton crew,
Cowering in their cushioned control seats.

Through the windows, the new world is revealed,
No longer a primal, barren wasteland,
But a green and blue and white avatar
Of our geoengineering prowess.

The new world's architect observes it all
From his throne at the foot of the windows,
Unperturbed by the rattling nanite clouds
As we rush through them at tremendous speed.

We do not seem to have broken orbit,
Which means Sigmund must be altering it.
Using railings, I haul myself across,
Fighting all the way against inertia.

The crew reach out to me, push me along,
Their skinny limbs not meant for these forces;
Some look as if they are struggling to breathe,
Clutching their armrests tight as they panic.

My own breath comes short. "What are you doing?"
I ask Sigmund, but he does not answer.
He does not need to – our destination
Is clear, visible on his monitor.

I recoil from the bright graphic display
Showing the route he has plotted for us.
He has put us on an intercept course
With the glittering moon – with New Terra.

"You're going to kill us all!" I tell him,
But he simply smiles at me, nods sagely.
"This was always the plan, Rochelle," he says.
"Our job is done. It's time for us to go."

I am breathless. "But what about the crew?"
My vision blurs as I begin to weep.
"They are tools, Rochelle. A means to an end.
If it helps, don't think of them as people."

"But they are people. And the New Terrans.
You and me, we're people as well," I say,
But Sigmund shakes his head and takes my hand;
"The colonists must never know of us."

I push past him and try the ship's controls,
And he tells me what I already know:
"Our destination is locked. But there's time
Enough for you to make peace with your god."

Panicking, I let myself fall backwards,
Sliding across the bridge to the tunnel.
Maybe I can find some other controls
Near the engines, and stop this disaster.

At the tunnel, I hear Sigmund calling.
"Thank you for everything, Rochelle!" he cries.
"I'm glad it was you, out of everyone.
Nobody else would have cared quite as much!"

The hill at the back of my father's church
Was always one of my favourite places.
Every single Sunday after service
I would mount that shallow mound by myself.

In autumn, the copse at the top would drip,
And the yellowing grasses would crunch, crisp,
And I would fill my fur-lined hood with leaves
Just to sift through all the sun-burned colours.

In winter, I would crack the frozen pond
Filled with beer cans at the base of the copse
By throwing little rocks at the hard white,
Watching my breath wisp, ghostly in the cold.

In spring, bluebells and snowdrops would emerge,
Followed by a gush of bright daffodils,
Among which the noisy magpies would dance,
And I would dance with them, watching them fly.

But summer – summer was always the best,
When the slopes would bloom in vivid colours;
Wild flowers humming so heavy with bees,
The trees so indulgently waxy green.

This was my place of prayer – better than church,
Making daisy-chain crowns and worshipping,
Giving thanks by making a tyre swing
And letting my laughter rise to heaven.

I went back, just before Jakob's passing.
The church was mouldering in disrepair,
But the hill was just as I had left it,
As if it was a prayer paused mid-sentence.

By that time, Jakob was nearing the end,
So fragile I was afraid to touch him.
I had to wheel him up the shallow slope,
His head so heavy it lolled against him.

Only his beard was the same as before:
That luscious black expanse, hiding his smile
As I showed him my childhood getaway,
Explaining all its hidden nuances.

I laid a blanket across his thin legs,
Helping him sip water from a cold flask,
Holding his delicate hand so lightly,
As if too much pressure might shatter him.

A few days later, Jakob would be dead,
Defeated by the cancer in his bones,
A warning to DNEs everywhere:
This is why you get inoculated.

That afternoon was our last together,
A moment of peace, love and reflection,
And if I concentrate on it enough,
I can still feel Jakob's hand gripping mine.

I concentrate on that sensation now.
Confronted, as I am, by my own death,
I reach out in memory to Jakob,
Asking him to lend me some of his strength.

The train breaks down halfway to the engines,
Leaving me stranded in a dark tunnel.
I force the door and step onto the tracks,
Using the sleepers as a guiding rail.

I am not sure how much longer I have,
But the engines are still so far away,
And I am only moving at a crawl,
Fighting against the fierce inertia.

There's a hatch and I breach it, crawling through,
Only to emerge in a long hallway
Composed, strangely, of mirror-plated walls;
I am reflected at me countlessly.

With my astronaut suit wreathed in flowers,
My features haggard, eyes brimming with tears,
The thousands of me turn about, helpless,
Trying to figure out some kind of plan.

Beyond the hall of mirrors is a park,
Walls painted to be vividly jolly;
The crew cower among the plastic plants,
Clutching onto each other for comfort.

I do not know how to help – what to say.
Should I tell them they are about to die?
There are children pressed up against the walls,
Already so frightened they are shaking.

At a junction between arched corridors
Where beyond the windows nanite clouds rush,
I spot an icon that I recognise:
There is a shuttle hangar close at hand.

By the time I stumble up to the door,
There is already a crush before it;
The crew are trying in vain to get through
The thick bulkheads shut so tight against them.

Of course the shuttle bays have been locked down:
The *Calypso* is meant to be our tomb;
Its tall walls no longer feel so spacious,
Lending it, instead, a funeral air.

Back at the junction, I see New Terra;
It has swung up across our horizon,
Now directly in the *Calypso*'s path;
That glittering moon which will end us all.

I have no time left to think, so I run,
Exoskeleton grinding painfully
As I force myself down a corridor
Towards the dark chamber at its apex.

Hauling the door open manually,
I climb inside the airlock, don my helm,
And try to initialise its cycle,
But of course the controls do not respond.

The glittering moon, so deadly, is close.
I tear at the emergency release
Until the metal covering comes free,
Then I wrench at the red lever beyond.

There is a series of bright explosions
Followed by an almighty force of air
As the room suddenly decompresses;
I tumble through the breach ripped in the door.

Surrounded by splinters of the airlock,
Tetherless, I tumble into the sky,
Vision whirling, hands grasping uselessly
As the *Calypso* accelerates past.

Her rockets are white flares, scarring my eyes,
Leaving burning streaks across my vision.
Only the sudden loss of inertia
Is a relief – I have become weightless.

Warning lights blink in my helmet's visor,
Telling me things that I already know:
I am spinning out of control in space,
And travelling at a tremendous speed.

I grab my wrist and jab at the panel,
Trying to remember my training drills;
This suit is clever, designed to save me
If I can recall the right sequences.

Micro-bursts hiss from my wrists and ankles,
Not enough to slow me down, but enough
To prevent me from endlessly spinning;
I turn myself to face the *Calypso*.

That colossal circlet reaches its end;
The glittering moon swinging towards her
Like a wrecking ball. I can only watch
As the *Calypso* and the moon collide.

I am struck, first, by the complete silence.
It lends the catastrophe a softness
As if both moon and ship are made of cloth;
Two cushions that might bounce from each other.

Yet neither object bounces – they both break;
The *Calypso* splinters and then explodes,
Cracking the moon's crust as its plasma drives
Release all their potential in one blast.

The sky is filled with pieces of them both.
The moon disintegrates, its shards spinning
Along with splinters of the *Calypso*;
Rock and metal detritus expanding.

Nothing on ship or moon could have survived.
The crew of the *Calypso* are all dead
Along with everyone on New Terra;
Sigmund's last act complete: twin genocides.

Yet I have little time in which to mourn:
My own orbit is pulling me quickly
Towards that expanding field of debris.
I curl up and try to make myself small.

Chunks of moon the size of small continents
Split and shatter into rocky islands,
While sharp shards of the *Calypso*'s bulkheads
Cut deadly spinning arcs across the sky.

Among all that catastrophe I fly,
So much faster than the debris's orbit
That I will be free of it in moments
Should I manage to avoid all of it.

I see a piece of a sarcophagus,
Cables writhing in its wake as it spins,
A remnant of those years I spent asleep
While the *Calypso* crossed the deep expanse.

I smash through a tangle of frozen vines,
Scattering stiffened leaves; I remember
The way that Catherine danced with her vines,
So happy to see that they had survived.

Archways and bulkheads splinter around me,
The *Calypso*'s corridors unfolding,
Revealing painted pieces of the parks
The crew constructed to simulate Earth.

A chunk of New Terra disintegrates,
Spilling silvery buildings through the sky,
So that I fly through broken tower blocks
Where dark corpses still cower in terror.

A dented projector illuminates
The crumbling remains of a corridor,
Flickering light showing a beach-side scene
Eclipsed by me as I plummet through it.

Beyond, there is more of the *Calypso*:
A mushroom farm billowing into space,
Its eerie tiered and ribbed contents glinting
With the sudden ice making them frosty.

I fall through a vivid green algae spew
Turning it to diamonds – facets shining,
All the time trying to ignore the fact
That I am surrounded by the dead crew.

      There are too many corpses to take count;
They are agonised rictus shapes scattered
As if the *Calypso* was a ripe fruit
And they are its seeds, dug out from its flesh.

      Then, all at once, I am free of the wreck,
Surrounded instead by the bright white sky,
Its nanite clouds threatening to consume me
As I continue my perilous flight.

      I turn and glimpse the wreckage one more time,
Moon and ship quickly disintegrating
Into a scattered amalgamation
That is neither ship nor moon any more.

      All of that ruination will orbit,
And perhaps, given some time, stabilise.
Like Saturn, the new world might wear a ring
Formed out of an ancient catastrophe.

      Almost at once the nanite clouds claim me,
So that I fly through a pale shadow realm
Surrounded on all sides by silhouettes
Shifting in the ethereal shimmer.

      If I had the time and the expertise
I could reprogramme some of the nanites
To reconstruct the collapsed *Calypso*,
Or at least a raft for me to land with.

      Instead, the nanites shimmer across me,
Sliding like quicksilver silk over me,
Reforming wherever they are disturbed
Into their radiant cloud formations.

All I have to survive in is my suit.
I suddenly feel tiny in the sky,
A small remnant of a catastrophe;
Insignificant at any distance.

   I fly free of the nanite clouds and there,
Gorgeously resplendent, is the new world,
Overwhelming me with its circumference
And all the verdant colours within it.

   Here, then, is where I must make my descent.
I raise my wrist-pad up to my visor,
Typing in the emergency commands
That were drilled into me during training.

   A warm hum reverberates down my spine,
Plates shift across my shoulders, and then burst,
Heralding the suit's metamorphosis.
No longer am I so small in the sky.

   My solar wings unfurl and catch the light,
Broad enough that they must brush against stars.
My shadow is cast vastly beneath me:
A dark shape on an errant nanite cloud.

   The new world's moons wheel in endless orbit
And I fly among them, now in control,
Gliding across the lattice of starshine
Enmeshed between the clouds, new world and sun.

   First, I use my wings to decelerate,
So that I am no longer hurtling quick
Through the perilous, glorious heavens;
Soaring instead at a sensible speed.

   Then, I search for a good path of descent,
Scouring the sky for pillars of sunshine
Bright enough to glide easily upon
And stable enough to keep me in flight.

There, ahead, I see a likely pillar
Cast through a broad gap in the nanite clouds
And illuminating the sparkling sea
Still so many fathoms distant to me.

Flying to avoid any eclipses
That might send me tumbling from the heavens,
I soar from shining beam to shining beam,
Suspended like a mote of dust on them.

The pillar of sunshine warms me greatly;
I am bathed in its luxurious light.
Solar wings strengthened by its radiance,
I arc across it, soaring so freely.

Wheeling bird-like, I circle the sunlight,
Angling my wings to commence my descent,
Gold foil feathers suspending me sweetly
As I pass through the last of the nanites.

At the edge of the new world's atmosphere
I feel its mighty gravity pull me,
Strengthening as I draw slowly closer,
Competing against the thrust of my wings.

Through that thin outer layer I descend,
The atmosphere gradually thickening,
Until I am among thin vapour clouds
So unlike the bright nanites in orbit.

I slow my descent as much as I can,
Drawn so fiercely towards the surface
By the new world's colossal gravity
That I have to seek the strongest sunshine.

Below me now is an unfocused green,
An expanse of hills and jagged mountains
Beside a shining mirror-glass ocean;
I try to steer myself towards the land.

Soon, trees begin to come into focus;
The canopies of the forests down there
Speckled with small avian silhouettes;
I try and mirror their fleeting movements.

I descend close enough to see streamlets
When at last a dark cloud rolls overhead,
Severing the light keeping me in flight.
My wings lose their tension – I start to fall.

Using my momentum, I try to glide,
Pitching forward over a canopy
Until I find enough of a glimmer
Upon which to suspend myself again.

The glimmer is no more than a moment;
An errant sparkle cast by a river;
But it is just enough to propel me
Towards a clearing in the thick forest.

The glow gone, I tumble ungracefully,
Drawn suddenly down to the hard surface,
Sliding and rolling across the grasses
And splintering my wings beneath myself.

I come to a sharp halt against a tree
And there I remain, with my heart pounding,
Breathing hard against the strong gravity
Until I feel ready to move again.

I sit up against the base of the tree,
Gently testing each of my limbs in turn,
And while I am bruised, nothing seems broken.
Somehow, I have survived the *Calypso*.

Through the break in the trees, I can see her:
A stream of ruination in the sky.
I watch the catastrophe as it arcs,
Following it until it vanishes.

I try to stand, but I am too weary,
So I shuffle in among the tree's roots.
Making myself comfortable, I lie back
And allow myself a few moments peace.
Catherine surrounds me completely, here.
I can feel her presence all around me.
Comforted by my friend, I catch my breath,
At last feeling my heart begin to slow.

Walk one last time with the man named Arthur Sigmund
Who is in Rome after burying his father.
The Sigmund estate was in complete disarray
Necessitating a whole month of untangling.
Arthur is exhausted, and it shows in his stride:
He meanders through the Vatican, unseeing
All the marvellous architecture around him,
Simply riding the waves of tourists pushing him;
Examining without seeing his tour pamphlet.
From time to time somebody recognises him,
Forcing him to stop, smile, shake hands and take pictures,
But otherwise he is left to his weary thoughts.
Eventually, he comes to the Sistine Chapel
And it is there he is finally roused from grief,
Confronted, as he is, by Michelangelo.
The frescos are still resplendent, even today,
Evocative, even encased behind perspex;
Reminiscent of the dead faith that inspired them.
Earlier in the year, Arthur met the people
Who are designing the *Calypso*'s colonists,
Imbuing them with all the properties they need
To survive the long journey across the expanse
And adapt to the atmosphere of the new world.
They will be a completely new kind of people,
Unaware of Earth, or their own humanity,
And it is those colonists that Arthur thinks of.
Here, in the Sistine Chapel, is a masterpiece,
But it feels so long since anybody made one;

These days – to Arthur – all art feels derivative,
Embedded inescapably in tradition,
Schools of thought, and thousands of years of history.
But the colonists, ignorant of history
Will have no such encumbrances on their thoughts;
They will be free to create their own works of art,
Inspired by their own completely new history;
They will be able to make new masterpieces
Inspired by whatever it is that inspires them.
Heartened by these thoughts, Sigmund exits the chapel
And walks through Rome, stride lengthened – if he hurries now
He will be able to arrive at the forum
In time to witness the *Calypso* eclipsing.
Searching through his pockets, he finds the pocketbook
Where he stored the one thing he kept from the estate,
Found there at the back of a cupboard in his room;
His childhood room, the walls still painted with rockets,
The cupboards still full of star-charts and telescopes.
At the forum, he stands in the ancient ruins
And unfolds the piece of paper from his notebook;
A thin piece of tracing paper, all yellowed now:
The only art that Arthur ever created.
It is nothing but a simple empty circle,
But to him it means so much – it is a symbol:
A wheel without spokes; a planet without people;
And there, in the dimming forum, he holds it up,
Covering the sun with the tracing paper curve,
And squinting hard through it to see if it aligns.
When he takes the tracing paper circle away,
Like a magic trick, the circle stays in the sky,
Intersecting the sun like a Venn diagram.
Everybody around Arthur is looking up,
Shielding their eyes with hands and special sunglasses
To see the *Calypso* up there, still skeletal,

Still with a few decades left of her construction,
But magnificent in orbit – a cathedral
Every bit as resplendent as the Vatican.
To Arthur, the *Calypso* is a dream come true.
She is his masterpiece, and it will be through her
That a new kind of people will be realised,
Freed, at last, from the chains of human history.

I never enjoyed my father's sermons.
His services were always passionate,
Delivered with absolute conviction
And welcomed by his small congregation.

Yet they were always so political;
Rooted in contemporary problems
Far beyond my childish understanding.
I failed to find inspiration in them.

What I enjoyed most was the time after,
Up on my sunny or icy hillside
When he would bring a blanket, sit with me
And tell me all about the son of God.

He did not always find the time for it.
Some weeks he would spend hours shaking hands
At the doorstep of his tiny parish
And stumble home, exhausted, afterwards.

So, each Sunday picnic became precious.
My father would come and find me, and sit,
And talk about Jesus like an old friend
Who he knew very well and saw sometimes.

Those lyrical and gentle afternoons
Slowly instilled my father's faith in me.
In that way, I think, he lives on in me,
Through the beloved stories he told me.

One time, he told me about Creation;
About God's loving act – making the Earth;
And that story, more than any other,
Ignited my young imagination.

I consider what it must have felt like
To dissolve and catalyse the new world.
Maybe it was like becoming a swarm:
Thinking with many minds instead of one.

If I close my eyes I feel so heavy,
Like my own body should disintegrate,
Infecting Catherine's new paradise
With my impure and corrupted innards.

I will die on this world, I realise.
With the *Calypso* and New Terra gone
I am trapped here for the rest of my life,
No matter how long or short it might be.

And then, I really will disintegrate:
The new world's carrion will peck at me,
The worms will devour me, and I will be
As much a part of this place as they are.

There is a certain comfort to that thought:
That I will be allowed to rot down here,
On dry land, and beneath an open sky,
Instead of eternally orbiting.

Hauling myself up and on to my feet
I navigate through the verdant forest,
Picking my way over pieces of wing
Scattered like slivers of golden sunshine.

Down an embankment, I come to a stream,
Its sleek surface serving as a mirror.
I kneel and see myself – the astronaut,
Her suit wound with vibrant plastic flowers.

Removing my helm, I construct a mask,
Remembering how Catherine did it,
Binding tubes to a layer of perspex
And moulding it so that it fits my face.

Without my suit, the new world will kill me:
I will never adapt to breathe the air.
Pulling the mask on, I inhale deeply
And the forest stops spinning around me.

Helm removed, I can feel a chilly breeze;
It tumbles my hair over my shoulders
And makes my teeth chatter – my limbs shiver.
Removing my gloves, I cup some water.

This water should be safe for me to drink
But I am still hesitant, watching it
For any sign that it might poison me.
It pools in my palms so deliciously.

Mask pulled aside, I sip and then I drink,
Raising more and more handfuls and gulping
Until it feels as if I am the stream,
Its length running so quickly down my throat.

Sated, I lay back down against the bank,
My suit humming as it starts to warm me,
Its heating systems kicking in to help
With the sudden onslaught of cold liquid.

I pat my pockets down, searching for things
That might help me survive on the new world,
Wishing that I had at all been prepared
For the fulfilment of Sigmund's vision.

In one pocket I find a carapace,
Those exoskeletal insect remains
From my meal of a mere few hours past.
It shimmers, ethereal in daylight.

And in another pocket, I find pills;
Two quicksilver rainbow-coloured capsules.
I hold them up to the light and shake them,
Watching the way the thick liquid oozes.

Without hesitation I swallow one,
Seeking some kind of relief from the thoughts
That are threatening to overwhelm me;
Perhaps a little clarity will help.

Then, I lay back again, and watch the sky,
Searching, in its massive blue openness
For a sign or some kind of direction
While I wait for the drug to take effect.

Clouds pass by, and I think of my father
The parables he would relate to me up on my hill
the way his face would fold up crease up in thought
his expression valleys and hills shifting
his lined face a map of love
all his love for me for God so clear;
on cold days he would shrug a blanket
rubbing fiercely at my arms
until my fingers prickled tingled;
on warm days he would remove his collar
let me play with it
a slip of white between my fingers
a blank sheet of paper
his throat exposed
Adam's apple bobbing
soft laughter, his laughter soft
as gentle as distant birdsong
the birds in the trees would quiet
listening, listening like me
do birds go to heaven?
I hope so, Chelly
so do I, Dad – I like their wings
will we fly in heaven?
my father's smile as soft as his laugh
we will be loved, Chelly
another story, about love compassion grace

all the good there is
I rise, rise from the riverbank
the sensation of a blanket tumbling from my shoulders
the ghost of a beloved memory
you will be loved, Chelly
I go down to the water
wade in, boots humming round my toes
plastic flowers unbound drift
I stride strong against the current
to a grove, I arrive
drooping trees laden with fruits
heavy with delicious cargo I pluck
morsels so sweet
digging seeds with my fingernails
I trench the embankments
planting more trees
tiny saplings rising instantly
Catherine's potent transformation still at work, unslowed
I bite, chew segments of her
through veils of leaved drapery
I part green curtained trees
deeper into the dusky grove
a doe skips the river, startling me
I turn and see all their eyes
beasts and fowl and fish they watch me
I laugh, in love so in love
this new world a paradise
I want to become water
become the river and sea and flow
as much the world as Catherine
I find the final capsule and raise it
an ode to my transformation
an overdose or a catalyst or both
not taken in fear but in joy I swallow

striding now faster up the stream I go
water thick with fishes
their scales brushing against my boots
I push my fingers in among them feel them
cold and slippery and so so real
iridescent remnants of my friend
I feel my thoughts start to
it's like a
everything is colour
not euphoria, but
the trees part and there am I
not I but she a colonist
absorbed in her own reflection
in a mirror-glass pool
a gasp, as she sees me
rising to her feet, eyes wide
and I
she doesn't run
I raise my hand
hello

ACKNOWLEDGEMENTS

First thanks must go to astronauts Tim Peake, Samantha Cristoforetti and Frank De Winne, who were each kind enough to share their experience of seeing the Earth from space with me. Those conversations informed and inspired much of this book.

I should also highlight the extraordinary work of George Sandison and Kev Eddy at Titan Books, both of whom checked and double-checked the metre of every single line. Darren Kerrigan was generous enough to work on this book with me, providing the illustrations that would become a part of the verse, and Julia Lloyd built on those illustrations to design a book that feels whole, and complete, and beautiful.

This book was written with the close eye of Colin Herd and Gavin Miller on it. Thanks, too, to Ruth E.J. Booth, Sally Gales, Gillean McDougall, Maria Sledmere, Dana Little, Amy Shea, Tawnya Renelle, Gillian Shirreffs, Elizabeth Reeder, Sophie Collins, Robert Maslen, Brian Atteberry and Carolyn Jess Cooke, all of whom provided feedback at critical points during the book's development.

Thank you to my agent, Alexander Cochran, and thanks to everyone at Titan – George Sandison and Michael Beale especially – for their belief in this book. And thank you to Tam Moules, who performed the Lords of New Terra section with me live at various events while the book was being written.

Thanks must also go to everyone at the European Space Agency who was kind enough to speak with me during my residency at the Astronaut Centre. Romain Charles, Aidan Cowley, Elena Filippazzo, Alison Koehler, Quinlan Buchlak, Angelos Alfatzis, Sabrina Alam, Rik Volger, Dorota Budzyn´, Hervé Stevenin, Lionel Ferra, Laura André-Boyet, Matt Day, Stéphane Ghiste and Andreas Diekmann all do extraordinary, inspiring work.

Finally: thank you to everyone who was generous enough to read through the earlier version of this book and offer their support for it. Without you, this beautiful finished edition would never have found its way to print.